Also by Alice Walker

FICTION

The Way Forward Is with a Broken Heart
By the Light of My Father's Smile
Possessing the Secret of Joy
The Temple of My Familiar
The Color Purple
You Can't Keep a Good Woman Down
Meridian
In Love and Trouble: Stories of Black Women
The Third Life of Grange Copeland

NONFICTION

Sent by Earth: A Message from the Grandmother Spirit
Anything We Love Can Be Saved
The Same River Twice: Honoring the Difficult
Warrior Marks (with Pratibha Parmar)
Living by the Word
In Search of Our Mothers' Gardens

POEMS

A Poem Traveled Down My Arm
Absolute Trust in the Goodness of the Earth
Her Blue Body Everything We Know
Horses Make a Landscape Look More Beautiful
Good Night, Willie Lee, I'll See You in the Morning
Revolutionary Petunias and Other Poems
Once

NOW IS
THE TIME
TO OPEN
YOUR HEART

RANDOM HOUSE

NEW YORK

NOW IS
THE TIME
TO OPEN
YOUR HEART

A NOVEL

Alice Walker

All rights reserved under International and Pan-American Copyright Conventions. Published in the United States by Random House, an imprint of The Random House Publishing Group, a division of Random House, Inc., New York, and simultaneously in Canada by Random House of Canada Limited, Toronto.

RANDOM HOUSE and colophon are registered trademarks of Random House, Inc.

Library of Congress Cataloging-in-Publication Data
Walker, Alice.
Now is the time to open your heart : a novel / Alice Walker.
p. cm.
ISBN 1-4000-6173-3
1. Self-actualization (Psychology)—Fiction. 2. Colorado River (Colo.-Mexico)—Fiction. 3. Separation (Psychology)—Fiction. 4. Amazon River Region—Fiction.
5. Shamanism—Fiction. 6. Travelers—Fiction. 7. Hawaii—Fiction. I. Title.
PS3573.A425N69 2004
813'.54—dc21   2003054766

The author is committed to preserving ancient forests and natural resources and wishes to acknowledge Random House for printing this book on paper that is 100 percent postconsumer recycled fibers and processed chlorine free. For more information about Green Press Initiative and the use of recycled paper in book publishing, visit www.greenpressinitiative.org.

Printed in the United States of America
Random House website address: www.randomhouse.com
9 8 7 6 5 4 3 2 1
First Edition
Book design by Victoria Wong

To Anunu and Enoba

Acknowledgments

With this writing, whatever its faults, I express my gratitude to all devas, angels, and bodhisattvas who accompany, watch over, and protect explorers, pioneers, and artists.

Everything in the universe has a purpose. There are no misfits, there are no freaks, there are no accidents. There are only things we don't understand.

—MARLO MORGAN, *Mutant Message Down Under*

So far, there is no law against dreaming.

—WINNIE MANDELA

My father's mother was murdered when he was a boy. Before she married my grandfather, Henry Clay Walker, her name was Kate Nelson. This novel is a memorial to the psychic explorer she might have become. It also made clear to me in the writing how much I miss her. And have always missed her.

*NOW IS
THE TIME
TO OPEN
YOUR HEART*

Cool Revolution

KATE TALKINGTREE SAT MEDITATING IN A LARGE hall that was surrounded by redwood trees. Although the deep shade of the trees usually kept the room quite cool, today was unseasonably warm and Kate, with everybody else, was beginning to perspire. They had been meditating, on and off their cushions, for most of the morning, beginning at five-thirty when they roused themselves, at the sound of the bell, from their beds. When they broke from meditating inside, they quietly made their way outside and into the courtyard. Up and down the path that led to the front door of the hall they did a walking meditation that had been taught them by a lot of different Buddhist teachers, some from America and some from Asia. It was a slow, graceful meditation that she liked; she enjoyed the feeling of a heel touching the earth long before a toe followed it. Meditating this way made her feel almost as slow as vegetation; it went well with her new name, a name she'd taken earlier, in the spring.

Ever since she was small she'd felt a wary futility about talking. At the same time she realized it was something that, in order for the world to understand itself at all, had to be done. Her old last name had been Nelson, and for a time she'd thought of calling herself Kate Nelson-Fir. She loved fir trees, especially the magnificent, towering ones that grew on the Northwest coast.

When it was time for the dharma talk to begin Kate made her way to a spot close enough to see and hear the teacher very easily. He was a middle-aged man of southern European descent, with an ecru complexion and a shining bald head. His brown eyes twinkled as he talked. Every once in a while he reached up and stroked the silver earring in his left ear. Because of the earring and because he seemed spotless in his flowing robes, she mentally dubbed him Mr. Clean. She had been coming to his talks every day for more than a week, and had enjoyed them very much. Today he was talking about the misguided notion that a "hot" revolution, with guns and violence, such as the ones attempted in Africa, Cuba, and the Caribbean, could ever succeed. He seemed unaware that these revolutions had been undermined not only by their own shortcomings but also by military interference from the United States. The only revolution that could possibly succeed, he maintained, smiling, was the "cool" one introduced to the world by the Lord Buddha, twenty-five hundred years ago.

Something about this statement did not sit well with Kate. She looked at him carefully. He was certainly a well-fed-looking soul, she thought. Not many meals missed by that one, except by accident. Quietly glancing down at the program on the floor beside her, she saw he had grown up in an upper-middle-class home, had had educated and cultured people as parents and as grandparents, had studied and lived in Europe as well as in the East. Was now a prominent professor at one of the country's most famous universities. Easy enough for him to dismiss the brown and black and yellow and poor white people all over the globe who worried constantly where their next meal was coming from, she thought. How they would feed, clothe, and educate their children. Who, if they did sit down to meditate, would probably be driven up again by the lash. Or by military death squads, or by hunger, or by . . . the list was long.

Looking around her she noticed most of the meditators shared the teacher's somewhat smug, well-fed look. They were overwhelmingly white and middle- to upper-middle-class and had the money and leisure time to be at a retreat. In fact, she noted, she seemed to be the only person of color there. What was wrong with this picture?

Her mind, which had been clear as a reflecting pool just minutes before, now became cloudy. This was exactly what meditation was meant to prevent. She took a deep breath, labeled her thoughts "thinking," as she'd been instructed to do if her mind wandered during meditation, and settled herself more firmly on her cushion. She would listen to this teacher, whom she indeed respected very much, and she would not be critical. Besides, she knew what he meant. There was a way in which all "hot" revolutions defeated themselves, because they spawned enemies. Look at those crazy ex-Cubans in Miami, for instance, who never recovered from having some of their power taken away, and the endless amount of confusion, pain, and suffering they caused.

After the talk she began to think in earnest. She felt she had reached an impasse on the Buddhist road.

That evening and the next day and the next she found herself unable to meditate. She kept looking out the window instead, just as she had looked out of the window of the Church of God and Christ, as a child, when she had been unable to believe human beings, simply by being born, had sinned. The redwood trees looked so restful, their long branches hanging down to the earth. Each tree created a little house, a shelter, around itself. Just right for a human or two to sit. She hadn't realized this before, how thoughtful this was. But on her very next walking meditation she slowly, slowly, made her way to the largest redwood tree and sat under it, becoming invisible to the dozens of people who continued their walking meditation and slowly walked all around her.

When everybody else returned to the meditation hall, she did not.

To Kill or to Thaw the Anaconda

SHE DREAMED SHE WAS EMPTYING HER FREEZER and there among the forgotten leftovers lay an alive but perfectly frozen anaconda. A huge orange and spotted snake, ashen, until she poured water on it and its ice sheeting began to melt; the color of the sun. She felt she must kill it before it thawed. She ran to others for help. None could help her; they were busy with their own lives. Their own anacondas. She cried out to one person after another: *Necesito ayuda! Puedo?* I need help! Can I help? She thought she was saying, Can *you* help? But she wasn't. Only on waking, all outside help refused her, did she realize dealing with the anaconda was an inside job. Whether to kill it or let it thaw and live was entirely up to her.

And wasn't she always saying what Grandmother Yagé had taught her: We are all on the back of a giant anaconda. It is slithering and sliding, darting and diving, like anacondas do. That is the reality of the world.

She woke up remembering a story from her days in the Black Freedom Movement. When she and her companions sought to encourage voting in a population that had been terrorized all their lives for trying to do so. An old woman had said

to them, as they walked their weary miles across Alabama and
Georgia and other outposts of the soon to be dubbed "New
South," Let me tell you a story about a man and a snake. They
put down their notepads and melting-in-their-hands pens, the
heat was so intense, and hiked up their jeans, took a seat on a
stump in her yard, and listened. She was so old she smelled like
greens. And so real a number of them swooned. There was this
man walking down the road, you see. And she pointed to the
long dirt road down which they had trudged, looking for her
house. And it was a very, very cold day. They looked into one
another's profusely perspiring faces and couldn't begin to imagine it. And what do you think he saw just ahead of him on the
road? Well, she carried on, without waiting for them to guess,
there right in his path was a snake. Kinda a cute snake. You
know, probably had hair like most people want and long eye-
lashes. Her audience smiled. It was frozen solid though, it was.
But still, some part of it could talk to the man. You know how
that is. They chuckled. And it said: Please, Mr. Man. I'm just a
poor little ole snake nearly 'bout froze to death out here in this
weather! Please take pity on me and warm me by putting me
in your bosom. Now, the man wasn't usually no fool. But you
know how it sometimes be. That one day, well. He thought
about it. And he was after all a Christian kind of a man. He
stood there thinking how amazing it was that such a cute snake
could talk. And then he stood there a good five or ten minutes
thinking about what Christ would do. If I was to pick you up,
he said, leaning over the snake so that his own shadow became
a part of it, and he, being a sensitive soul, started to feel a connection, If I was to pick you up, how do I know you wouldn't
bite me? Oh, no, Mr. Man, if you would be so kind as to warm
me up and let me live, why, it would be a horrible thing for me

to repay your kindness by biting you! I wouldn't dream of such a thing.

So after a while, the snake looking at him so pitiful, he picked the little ole thing up, and he put it in his bosom, in the pocket of his overalls. Just behind his package of Brown Mule chewing tobacca and right next to his chest, close to his heart, which was beating warming blood all through his sympathetic body. And they walked on. The man thinking real good things about himself and the little snake beginning to feel like him or her self again. Pretty soon the snake was warmed clear through. The man could feel it slowly uncoiling, slithering behind his hansker pocket just a tiny bit. It make him smile, to tell you the truth. It tickled him to think that something as humble as himself could bring something frozen almost dead practically back to life. He reached up to pat the snake. And the snake bit him.

He bit him on the jaw. And the man knew he was in the middle of Alabama or Mississippi or Georgia or north Florida or somewhere there wasn't likely to be no speedy help. He fell down in the middle of the road, just a cussin'. Why you do me like that? he asked the snake, who was now sliding nimbly across his pants leg. And the snake looked up at him and said, kind of shrugging his shoulders like those folks in France do: You knowed I was a snake when you picked me up. And the man started to die.

The old woman looked at the young people who had disturbed her peace to ask her to join their crusade. She had learned to live without picking up any snakes. She killed every one she saw, no hesitation and no questions asked. She did have a different ending for the story though, that she felt might do them good; for she could see they were understanding her to say what they were attempting was an exercise in futility.

She cleared her throat, which had as many wrinkles as the ocean has waves. Now listen, though, she said, most people stop that story right there. They act like the man was just a total fool, outsmarted one more time, like ole Adam. But when you think more about the story, about the man and the weather and the snake, you understand it differently.

How's that? someone from the group asked dejectedly. They had walked all morning in the broiling sun just to be told they were picking up something whose bite would eventually kill them.

Well, said the old woman, think about the weather. It was still real cold. That snake, he was gonna freeze again. Once he froze again, he'd be helpless again. No kind of protection for a snake too froze to bite.

So? asked the same person.

So, said the old woman, this is an endless kind of a thing. Do we kill it or do we let it live? Do we ever believe its true nature and does that true nature ever change? And does ours?

She had given them some grapes that grew out behind her house. And some water from her spring. Bye, she'd waved to them, as contented as a girl.

Change

SHE HAD DISMANTLED HER ALTAR. THE CANDLES, plentiful and varied, honoring deities from the Virgen de Guadalupe to Che, Jesus to her friend Sarah Jane, who'd been shot to death by death squads in Honduras, rested now in a large box beside the door. Her imposing poster of the languid and regal Quan Yin was rolled up and secured with a blue string, her classical Buddha who had begun to look like Ram Dass on acid she had draped with a purple cloth.

Her life was changing. She had felt it begin to shift beneath her feet. Or above her feet, because the change had started in her knees. In her fifty-seventh year they had, both of them, mysteriously, out of the blue, begun to creak.

At first she thought it was her shoes, an ancient pair of running shoes, noiseless as morning until then. Perhaps it was an article of clothing closer to her ear. But no, it was her knees. They creaked like unoiled door hinges. No bird, flying beside her as she ran, could make such a squawk. It seemed terrible to her. A failing of her always so quiet and unobtrusive body. The body of a farm girl—sturdy, peasant dependable—but also the body of a dancer—ever graceful, gliding through her days. But no more.

To her ears now every move was announced. She was unnerved.

She went, as soon as she could fathom where to go, to visit a knee specialist. To a woman who worked on the joints of athletes. This woman manipulated her knees, her legs, frowned, and ended the session by telling her to stretch every morning. To bring her calves to rest on the countertop in her kitchen while the coffee perked. Furthermore, said this woman, it would probably be useful if you invested in orthotics.

She did. And soon felt balanced, for the first time, perhaps, in her life. Until the constant change of shoes, the need to wear sandals in summer, the urge to walk barefoot on the beach, and in her own yard, stopped her. After this, wrenching pain in her hips, as her body sought to realign itself in patterns it had always known.

Her lover was still supple enough never to have experienced an ache in any part of his body except his head. He'd never experienced a creak anywhere. He was so inexperienced he could not hear her creakiness. He failed to grasp why such a small thing unsettled her. She, surely one of the people born "a big strong woman," such as Holly Near sang about. She wanted kisses on her knees that he could not remember to offer; nor could he understand, exactly, why kisses should be needed. It boded ill for them.

The lover before him would have understood perfectly. A woman closer to her own age, this lover had been capable of endlessly babying her, of kissing any bruise or pain, no matter how slight. Alas, she had soon enough felt smothered, and flown the too cozy nest. Still, at times like this, she missed having a lover who could feel, empathize with, her aging body.

She had dismantled her altar. Even the photographs of her parents—her mother radiant as a sun, her father glowing as a moon—she had taken down. They now were on the floor, facing the mud-colored wall. For hours she had sat gazing into their beloved faces; all criticism of them forgotten; all complaints exhausted. Nothing remained but love. Not even desire to see them again remained; and she had been disconsolate when they had both died suddenly, when a train rammed their car, and she'd spent years thinking she might turn a corner somewhere and see them, catch up to them, as it were, because, curiously, in her imagination, they were always on a path ahead of her; she saw their backs, dissolving around a long curve in the trail.

This room, her altar room, resembled a cave. Dark and quiet, like being in the earth, and the candles had been like a hearth, a fire pit, beckoning one to come forward and sit.

This was no longer the case. All now was in disarray. Her surroundings mirrored a dissolution she felt growing inside herself. And though she had loved her home, her berry-colored house with starry blue trim, she thought frequently of selling it. She even thought of giving it away. It did not seem important, though for years she'd jumped for joy each time she managed to pay the mortgage or to add some small or large improvement. Now she dreaded thinking about its needs. She noticed a shabbiness creeping in, she who had been so fastidious and never left a single broken thing unrepaired. She found she cared little that the paint over the fireplace was beginning to peel, that the door to the kitchen didn't quite close. That there was a leak beside the bathtub drain. She even thought about these things positively, in some new and quite weird way. She could feel her house dissolving around her, as her parents dissolved when she daydreamed them. And there was a feeling of relaxing, of letting go, that was welcome.

Every word she wrote now she thought of burning. Old

journals she gathered in a pile. To save in already overstuffed cupboards? Or to burn? And one day, ceremonially, she burned not only some of her writing but several hundred-dollar bills, just to demonstrate to herself that these items were not the God/Goddess of her life. Her friends grew quite alarmed. She began to dream each and every night that there was a river. But it was dry. There she'd be in the middle of an ancient forest searching for her life, i.e., the river, and she would find it after a long journey, and it would be sand.

Her pens as well seemed to go empty on her. An unusual number of them, though practically brand new, refused to scratch more than a few pale lines. No matter that she banged them in frustration on the desktop. Her eyes dimmed. Nor could her new reading glasses often be found. Was it the end? she thought. Or what?

And so her friends—the ones in her psyche and the ones sitting around her dining table—said: You must find a real river somewhere in the world—forget the dry one in your dreams— to travel down. They suggested one of the deepest, swiftest, most challenging of all: the Colorado.

She went. Taking just her light duffel of hiking and sleeping gear, mosquito repellant, aspirin, and a walking stick a friend had carved from a twig, lovely in its lightness and the color of dried hemp, she started on this journey. They had told her the river was wide. They had told her it was cold and deep. They had told her it roared through the Grand Canyon like a locomotive. They had forgotten to mention there were rapids. And so, the night before the start of the river run, in a motel room not far from the Grand Canyon's rim, reading at last the material that had been sent to her by the able women who would steer her boat and the boats of the nine other women journeying also, she sat bolt upright in bed, startling her companion, a friend of many kind and unkind years. *Merde,* she said (though she was not French or of that ancestry); there are rapids involved!

Not small, barely perceptible ripples on the river, but mighty upheavals of the river itself. The river, in fact, with its twenty- and thirty-foot waves, roiling beneath their tiny wooden dories, would attempt, daily, to dislodge them. She, having read about this, barely slept. And yet, it did not occur to her to turn back.

When she did sleep, for a few blissful minutes just before dawn, at which time they were to leave the motel, she dreamed she was in a high-rise building, living there, and that she was informed it was time for the water to rise. She thought this meant the water would rise perhaps to the level of the gutter outside the front door. But no, a cheerful dark woman waved from the control room of the global water department, high above her own dwelling, and, pulling a lever, instigated a flow of dark water, so dark a water it resembled oil, and all the floors beneath her were soon submerged. And then her own flat was flooded. She wondered of course if she would drown. But apparently not: By some fate she seemed to swim well in oil and water and she marveled that in the world of nondream these two were said not to mix.

She whispered her dream to her buddy Avoa. Who yawned, smiled at her, and said: Hmmm. Oil and water. Both. Sounds refreshing and rich. Before disappearing into the shower. Kate lay abed a few moments longer, musing.

Her lover, Yolo, had watched her leave. A compact, muscular woman with good skin and creamy white teeth, a woman no longer sure there was a path through life or how indeed to follow one if there was. He'd folded her in his arms, yawning as he stretched her slightly backward. It was already over between them. Both of them felt it. Her journey now was to be with women. Only women. Because of women. And partly because she had seemed to feel, and to wonder aloud, about the possibility that only women, these days, dreamed of rivers, and were alarmed that they were dry.

He had no such dreams, certainly. And if he had them, he did not recall them on rising. Nor could he fathom why this should be so. In fact, dreams, the world of dreams, did not exist for him as it existed for her. And unlike her, he did not sit before the dwindling fire of their hearth wondering, pondering, nagging the question really, What does this mean?

And she left. He watched the green shuttle stop, the driver lift in her gear, her sleep-creased face appear in a window. Then with a wave, a rapping of her stick against the pane, she was gone. He would have driven her to the airport had she wanted it. But no, she had wanted to leave her house heading directly into her journey. No long cuddles near the ticket counter, no second thoughts about whether they would be all right. It was like her to want it this way. No fuss. She would meet up with Avoa on the way, perhaps in Phoenix, and then the two of them would be off, as they seemed to manage to do now just about every year.

And feeling somewhat abandoned, *left*, he indulged his critical mind: She was not much of a housekeeper. He thought this while picking up one of his socks he'd discarded near the door. And grimaced at the inner critic. See, he said aloud, what do you know? He went inside the house, and while making a cup of coffee noticed a cobweb already beginning to attach itself to his cup. It made him laugh. To him, this was the way of Life. Turn your back for only a moment while the water boils and you are lost in the scent of things to come, and Life puts out a tentacle to grab some part of you. Even the cup from which you prepare to drink is already being pulled if only so slightly back to the ground. A ground that moves, changes, endlessly, but is, paradoxically, always the same. Or it had been the same until, as the old ones used to say, here lately. These "old ones" were, generally speaking, her old ones, but she shared them with him; a quaintness of expression, a drollness of thought, that she seemed to garner directly from her dreams. She might awake laughing anytime whether day or night and expose him to frolicsome goings-on, pithy sayings, the oddest *bon mot* from perhaps a century or so ago. Sometimes he'd cry: "I don't get it." And she'd laugh harder and say: "Well, I guess you'd just have to have been there!"

He would miss her. He already did so. Nothing to do, immediately, but go back to bed. To burrow under a comforter still warm from her body, still fragrant with her always fresh, slightly spicy scent. In a room in which there were always flowers, and candles, and a feel of the music that she so often played. Haydn and Beethoven, of course, and also the Beatles, Robbie Robertson and Red Road, and always and for endless hours, Sade and Al Green. Because *they* know how to love! she cried.

Drifting off into a minor squall of despair, an eddy of disappointment, and while hugging her pillow with the mixed emotions of loss, lust, and resentment, he fell asleep. And began immediately to dream. There is a path just ahead of him. Now he sees a large brown foot, hesitant, upon it. A green hobbitlike creature sits on its big toe, riding it as if it were a pony. The toe turns into a side trail. The trail disappears in the brush. The hobbit creature vanishes from sight, his green eyes, like his green leafy cap, sparkling. *You are lost, my boy,* the spirit being says.

Wait! he calls. *Which way to the river?*

His own shout, and the desperation with which he calls out, awakens him. He lies cradling her pillow, suddenly knowing it isn't over between them. That it will now never be, no matter that they may soon part. He has somehow joined her journey.

Hallelujah, he shouts, flinging aside the comforter, kicking away the covering quilt, giving her pillow a loud smack of a kiss, and heading jubilantly for the shower.

It blesses him. Never before, he feels, has he understood water. It cascades down his tight, healthy skin, and covers him, where the sun falls, with crystal beads of light. It astonishes him that in its purity, in its speed in covering his body, it has no scent. He smells only himself, earthy, rich, a friendly scent, he thinks, bemused, and the soap he holds, which is lemony. Also earthy, he thinks.

He thinks of how they met. She'd pursued him. After seeing one of his paintings of the desert. How can it move me so, she'd cried, gazing in rapture at a large canvas on which there was little other than space, sky, brown earth, and a large cactus. It is so empty!

Because emptiness, space, is our true home? he'd replied, amused by her enthusiasm, and that she'd called in the middle of the night to again pose the question.

It is, isn't it? she'd said, after a long pause. And the blue of your sky! she said.

He'd turned over in bed, happy not to have a wife beside him to disturb, and lit a cigarette. The habit of smoking (terrible, dumber than stupid, he knew) had taught him about emptiness, the need to fill internal space, the huge internal space existing within all of us, with Something. He was grateful he could smoke. Though he knew there were women who dismissed him the instant they saw him light up, because they could not imagine kissing him.

Do you know what O'Keeffe says about blue? he asked her, blowing out a cloud of smoke, warming to her voice, though he did not remember her face clearly from the opening night's exhibition.

What?

That it is the color that will remain after everything is destroyed.

He could feel her thinking. Savoring this idea. Her mind carrying her into the far reaches of the heavens, of space, long after there was no more earth.

But if we're not here to see it, she finally asked, will it still be blue?

He laughed, and asked her where she lived.

He recognized her immediately when he saw her again. And what he recognized was her energy, which seemed to precede her. As if her spirit were thrusting itself forward, into the unknown; dazzled, charmed, challenged, hopeful, happy to be energized by the mysterious, loving the adrenaline rush of surprise.

She was some years older than him and made no pretense of being younger. Her hair was graying; she would tell him later she was the sort who forgot to dye it, even when she tried to remember. She also felt humiliated to be eradicating some part of her hard-won existence. Don't people who try to look younger miss part of their lives? she queried, seriously. She also held a superstition she didn't tell him: that if you lied about your age, the number of years you took off were subtracted by the Universe. That's why so many people died sooner than they thought they would. She had her adequate cushion of estrogen fat on tummy and hips; her full breasts swung lower than ever before; her eyes sparkled to find herself still vitally alive. An artist who was passionately enchanted by the real, however odd or *singular* it might be, he felt, almost at once, a sense of home. They stood, at that first meeting, simply measuring each other with their eyes. They were nearly equal in height. He thought, immediately, of what a boon that would be for kissing. If, in fact, she deigned to kiss a smoker. He thought it might prove a boon for other things. But he was modest, and tried, unsuccessfully, not to go there.

She offered him tea. And a peach that seemed to materialize, like a hare from a hat, out of the green velvet sleeve of her embroidered shirt.

And it had begun.

We met, really, she would tell friends later, laughing, over nothing. Over emptiness. Space. I couldn't believe how much of it he managed to get into his paintings, or how at home I felt in it.

He'd smiled to hear her describe it.

The moment I stood in front of any one of his paintings, she elaborated, my bird nature became activated. I felt I could fly!

Her bird nature? Where had he been, and with whom had he been, not to know there were people, women, who talked this way?

She must be New Age, he'd thought at first, shuddering.

River Run

PERHAPS ON THE FIRST DAY OF ANY RIVER TRAVEL one is apprehensive, one feels fear. She sat with her African-Eurasian friend Avoa, deep in the boat, not liking the heaviness of the life preserver, poppy orange, around her neck. The river, at the place they put on, was placid. Nonetheless she could feel its power in the swiftness with which the vehicles that brought their gear disappeared, as did, very soon, the flat and gravelly shore.

Large birds flew ahead of them toward the canyons, wheeling as they appeared and disappeared from view. Tentatively she placed a hand in the water. Icy cold. While overhead the sun rose higher in the sky, already warm, almost hot.

They were to be on the river nearly three weeks, long enough to traverse its entire length. Who would she be at the end of this journey?

Why are you going? her therapist had asked.

And she had sat looking behind her therapist's head, scanning the posters of horses on the wall, and replied:

I cannot believe my dry river, that we have been discussing

for months, and that is inside me, is unconnected to a wet one somewhere on the earth. I am being called, she said.

But the Colorado? Isn't it man-made?

In the beginning, no, she said, laughing to think of early man creating so mysterious and powerful a thing as a river. It is the river after all that carved the Grand Canyon.

But now, pursued the therapist, isn't it controlled by dams?

Controlled? I think not. Regulated? Maybe. Though she did not know this either. She admitted to being the kind of traveler who didn't prepare much before taking off. She'd found something to enjoy in her own ignorance. Oh, that's who's in that tomb! That's why they wear waist beads! Oh, now I understand all those thick dark garments in this heat. It's like carrying your own shadow and your shade! In the back of her mind she was already wondering if she would learn anything about how the Colorado's water managed to fill the bathtubs and swimming pools in Los Angeles. How was that possible? And what happens to a river—even a man-enhanced one—that flows continuously to a desert?

On the fourth day, and after experiencing her first rapids— her boat pitched higher than a house—she became ill. As the boat pitched and plunged down the river she felt herself slipping into the surrealness of a life lived now in a tiny bobbing space, very narrow, within the steep reddish canyon walls. Rushing madly, irresistibly onward, no stopping it. Yet at the end of each day they did stop. And on the evening of this particular day they stopped longer than usual to confer with her. Her temperature was 104. Did she wish to be evacuated? They could manage somehow to get a helicopter for her. Did she wish to go home?

The savage rushing of the river seemed to be inside her head, inside her body. Even while the oarswomen, their guides, were speaking to her, she had the impression she couldn't quite hear them because of the roar. Not of the river that did indeed roar, just behind them, close to the simple shelter they'd made for her, but because of an internal roar as of the sound of a massive accumulation of words, spoken all at once, but collected over a lifetime, now trying to leave her body. As they rose to her lips, and in response to the question: Do you want to go home? she leaned over a patch of yellow grass near her elbow and threw up.

All the words from decades of her life filled her throat. Words she had said or had imagined saying or had swallowed before saying to her father, dead these many years. All the words to her mother. To her husbands. Children. Lovers. The words shouted back at the television set, spreading its virus of mental confusion.

Once begun, the retching went on and on. She would stop, gasping for breath, rest a minute, and be off again. Draining her body of precious fluid, alarming Avoa and the oarswomen. Soon, exhausted, she was done.

No, she had said weakly, I don't want to go home. I'll be all right now.

Avoa's eyes were huge. Kate realized she must look a fright. She took the electrolyted water offered her, and later on, a tepid broth.

Really, she said, attempting to smile. I'll be fine.

All the women looked skeptical, but helped Avoa set up a proper camp.

He Wondered

HE WONDERED, WANDERING ABOUT THE HOUSE, how she knew what to throw out and what to keep. Her house had a bare look. There was nothing extra. Yet she was one of those people who seemed to attract gifts and to buy them for herself. Nothing, however, stuck for long.

The rug rolled up by the door, for instance. A rug given her by a friend from Yugoslavia, when the people still had a country and enough of their wits about them to make traditional handmade rugs. A rug she'd loved for years. But now did not.

How did this happen?

He was the kind of person who kept things forever. His smaller house, a few blocks from hers, was filled with clutter. Each year for Kwanza she'd given him the same present: a book called *Clear Your Clutter with Feng Shui*. Each year he read it from start to finish. Each year he agreed with everything its author said—from the necessity of clearing one's front entrance, in order that a cleaner, more brisk energy might sweep through one's life—to the need to completely void and scrub out the colon, so that fresh life could sweep through the body. Think of all the old shit everyone's carrying around! she might say, raising her eyebrows in concern.

They might lie on the sofa—a large, overstuffed one built for two, their feet touching. Each reading silently. He might feel her eyes on him as he read, sometimes marking a page by turning back a corner. She might smile knowingly, hopefully. He might feel a surge of determination. Indeed, reading of all the ill effects of clutter—procrastination, lost items, fuzzy thinking—he might imagine his house already clutter-free.

And then he would return to his house and freshly see his clutter. The exercise bike that was covered in dust, the back issues of *Prevention* and *Utne Reader* resting beside the door. Bundles of clothes almost on their way to Goodwill. Chipped dishes. He did not use these things anymore, and yet, the thought of letting them go made him sad. He felt they represented times in his life he could not recall without their presence. They represented stories.

For had he not bought the exercise bike when he was in love with a leggy Swede and wanted to impress her with his fitness? Without the dusty machine to remind him, these days he'd never think of her. And that time too had been a real and vivid part of his life. At least at the time. And when he'd suddenly realized his body was changing. Aging. Perhaps needing supplements and vitamins, and he'd subscribed to *Prevention*. And then not long after had felt his disconnection from "the news" and the voices of "the media," and he'd subscribed to *Utne Reader*. And for a time had read it cover to cover every month. He was the only man he knew who owned a twelve-year-tall stack of *Ms.* magazine. The very first issue, in the early seventies, with a bluish painting of Shakti, her seven or so arms spinning, had caught his attention. He'd stood at a newsstand in New York City, furtively reading the thoughts of women, realizing he'd never known a thing about women his whole life. Looking back to that moment, he could not imagine becoming the man in Kate's bed without that experience.

He owned several clocks. For when their batteries failed he forgot that was the reason they stopped. Seeing some other clock and fancying it, he bought it. He bought shoes he already had. Underwear too.

Deep down he actually thought time had stopped. The clocks, then, were mementos, trinkets. Curios. Reminders of a time when people still lived and behaved as if they were going somewhere. Somewhere important. We are the Kings of the Universe was the internal mantra of almost everyone. And we are on a mission to Something, Someplace, better.

Not so. And now most people knew. Would the end be brutish and short? Or would it be long and drawn out? People dying slowly of every illness under the sun. From viruses that seeped from under jungle rocks. From infections received while making love. From fratricide. Genocide. Hatred that intensified over decades, centuries, until nothing could stop its rolling over and flattening entire peoples, races, continents. Would the passion and joy of future generations be expressed in acts of hate, as acts of "sex" were now routinely expressed in acts of violence?

The indigenous Australians thought Time was synonymous with Forever and that therefore it was ridiculous to wear it on your arm. Or to think one's short present lifetime made much of an impression on Time at all.

It was over, he thought, the kind of Time watches measured. We should all throw them away. He didn't though. He bought more. So that when he looked about his cluttered rooms, with their assortment of rundown clocks, he understood he had, by buying them, been attempting to preserve time, to hoard it.

I am a fool, he thought, observing this. And yet he continued to buy any timepiece that appealed to him.

While she was regurgitating over her left forearm into the yellowed grass and dusty olive green bushes, she thought of a serving dish her first husband and their child had given her for Valentine's Day. It had been a lively red and covered with white flowers. It was these white flowers, dozens of them, that now poured from her mouth. At the time of the gift she'd stuffed her disappointment. That she was now perceived as someone who, on a day especially set aside to celebrate lovers, could be enraptured to receive a serving dish.

Look at the roses! the child had cried.

Her husband had beamed at her. They'd chosen it together, he declared.

She had forced a smile she drew out of the thin air just behind her head. And she had said patiently, with kindness, to the child: No, they are daisies.

And he had said: Aren't they vibrant?

And she had replied: Yes, they are.

But all the time she was thinking: Am I so old now? Is the life that has Cupid in it, not to mention Eros, over for me?

And she began to think of the labor it sometimes was for her now to make love.

A lump had risen in her throat. Of sadness. Of disappointment. Anger that she had entered the unromantic era of life, so soon! That her child was in cahoots with her father in giving her this awful gift, this mirror in which she saw herself as someone whom time was passing by.

More years passed, and she stayed with them, and she saw how they ceased to really see her. They saw instead a service, a servant. And she'd gazed into their greedy eyes and saw the rest of her life being sucked away. And she had swallowed and swallowed.

Well. There it lay now, stinking in the sun beside one of the mightiest rivers on earth. The mass of rotten, once vibrant but artificial flowers, thrust upon her as a compliment when she had, in her soul, felt much too young, much too alive in her subterranean depths, to receive them. The pretense had been heavy as a car.

And to think how she had lain under him, night after night, dreaming of getting away; of being high on a hillside in the sun. Her wings grown back, her brows smooth and black above eyes that welcomed space, nothingness, in place of the domesticated, bourgeois life of a way that no longer fit.

The women were gentle with her. Placing all her small belongings—toothbrush and paste, soap, eyeglasses—within her reach.

Of what are you thinking? asked Avoa.

I am thinking of the moment something dies and how we instinctively know it. And of how we try not to know what we know because we do not yet understand how we are to negotiate change.

From death back into life?

From death, being dead, back into life, yes, she said.

Each night the crew set up the Porta Potti latrine in the most exquisite location imaginable. Tonight, under a huge canopy of stars, she sat like a queen, the flashing, roaring river silver in the moonlight. She thought of how diligently she'd worked to free herself. Difficult because of the shock she was in, discovering she was trapped. Captured most of all by possessions.

They'd bought a fairly large house, two floors, seven rooms, every one of which had to be filled. She groaned, now on the toilet, thinking about it. And yet they'd both rushed to the task. Buying things. It had excited them. Rug after perfect rug they'd bought. They'd bought silver. And linens. Chairs. A dining set. At some point, she thought, but wasn't sure, an electric knife. Now she couldn't imagine owning or using one. And they'd bought couches and lamps and footrests and stools and more art than she cared to recall. She had loved it, the art, more than anything else. Yet when she knew she must leave, the art became the heaviest purchase. He loved it too. And how do you divide a Matisse, even if it is only a print?

The heaving sickness past, her nausea gone, her bodily fluids replaced, she felt the lightness of being in the open space around her. Her walls the canyon's walls, she owned them not at all; her floor, the river beach. Her view, the heavens. It was, this freedom she was in, the longed-for cathedral of her dreams.

You will come back so different, Yolo had said, before she left on her journey, holding her loosely about the waist and gazing down at her. For months he'd felt, every time he held her, a kind of humming coming from her body. A buzzing. Energy being amassed, stored, building to the bursting point. And yet, when he mentioned this to her she said she felt no such activity. She felt instead dull, lethargic, as though she were solid, stuck.

Not so, he'd insisted. Your molecules are singing.

I don't hear them, she'd drily replied.

And if I change? she'd asked, looking at him intently, wanting to catch his most instinctive response. What will that mean to you? To herself she was thinking: Of course I will change; at least I hope so. Pray so. Without changing I will be doomed to stay my present self and I'm so weary of that!

I will still adore you, he said, kissing the top of her head. Only more so, probably.

She laughed. As he did so often, he'd offered the best possible response. It freed her. Now she could imagine a return. She saw herself flying back home, swooping in through a window, a large black bird. Transformed. Still welcome. Now she could go.

She mentioned to the oarswomen, but no more than that, the diarrhea. As her body spasmed and cramped and the precious fluids she was being given by Avoa disappeared into the elegantly situated latrine, she thought of the French characterization (she'd read it in an Englishman's book) of the English as people with a "talent" for diarrhea. Always, when they travel, getting it, having it, or looking for a place to have it. It humanized the English in a way that tickled her and so she smiled, even as she felt concern about her dizziness. She would not go home, though. Returning before ending her sojourn on the river was out of the question.

She left the latrine, gazed with adoration at the full moon rising just above the canyon's rim, leaning for several moments on her stick, and felt a peace—fleeting—she had not felt in years.

For her life, like human life everywhere on the planet, had speeded up and speeded up until peace was rarely possible. Always there was movement, noise, inevitable and constant distraction. Even if you managed to steal a day of quiet and expected no one to call the quiet place you had chosen, there would be the harsh ring of the phone you forgot to unplug and a solicitous voice—not the voice of one's children or lover—asking you to subscribe to a newspaper or to change your telephone service. A madness had seized earth. The madness of speed. As if to speed things up meant to actually go somewhere. And where, after all, was there to go? The present is all there ever is, no matter how you lean forward or back. Standing beside the river, realizing that the water of earth is recycled forever, she deeply understood this: that there are two "presents." One is of the moment. The other is of a longer moment—the "moment" that includes the history and knowledge one knows. So that, she mused, if the tears shed by the mother of Isis are now part of this river then I am somehow connected to her in this longer "present" that I am able to envision and that contains both of us.

A straw had stuck in one of her waterproof sandals. She bent to pull it out. It was the sundried spike of a yellow flower. The voice of her body urged her to put it into her mouth. To chew it. She did so. Immediately her stomach calmed. The dizziness left her.

Was it wild chamomile, she wondered.

What is this called? she asked the oarswoman of their boat.

At the moment that she asked, the woman, frowning, did not recall the flower's name.

And she realized she did not care. She did not need to know the name humans had given the flower. To herself she called it friend and from then on looked for it along the banks of the river and felt concern for its health.

That husband had shoved her in the back when she told him she was leaving. They had been hiking in the mountains when she told him; she was just ahead of him on a particularly rough part of the trail. Jagged rocks had been pushed up during the last winter; some so sharp she felt they might pierce the soles of her stout walking boots. They skirted a ravine, and a drop of more than two hundred feet was to their immediate right. She had been working up to telling him gradually; later on she would almost smile to think how like a coward she'd started out feigning cheerfulness down in the flatland, near the parking lot. She'd even rapped their trusty gray Dodge smartly as they were leaving, a signal that it was to be there, trusty as ever, when they returned. He'd smiled at her good-luck knock, and they'd felt companionable; at least she had felt that way. She'd wanted to talk, she'd said, and he'd suggested combining it with a hike through mountains they'd hiked often before the children came.

I don't see how we can go on like this, she'd muttered over her shoulder, as they climbed. He could barely hear her.

What? What did you say? he called, as she, always more nimble climbing than he, moved easily ahead.

I need more of my own life, she replied.

Your what? he said.

They'd stopped for breath. Admired the majestic view. She'd taken off her hat, shaken out her locks. Her back was still to him as they resumed.

I need to live alone, she said.

She felt him stop. She paused and was about to turn, and he, at the same moment, pushed her. It was a blow, but with the flat of his hand, against the small of her back. She scrambled to keep her footing on the narrow ledge. She might have fallen to her death. Steadying herself she turned to face him; he was staring at her as if she'd turned into his worst enemy.

She very carefully relieved herself of the backpack she was carrying, old and mauve and endearingly worn. She'd had it, she thought, even before she met him. And when she'd run off from the dorm to spend nights with him, she'd packed nightgown and toothbrush, jeans and a change of panties, in it. He'd told her she needn't bring a nightgown. She had though, because the backpack felt ridiculously light and flat without the flannel nightgown as filler. Besides, he'd liked to peel the old-fashioned thing off her. He'd also liked to dive underneath it and rest his face between her thighs.

Ah, she thought. Placing the memory at her feet.

Do you realize, she said to him, that I have lived with you for nine years. That I have carried in my body two of your children. That I have cooked thousands of breakfasts and lunches and dinners for you. That I have sat up with you when you've been sick. That I have helped you care for your parents. That I have shared my body with you whenever you wanted it, whether I felt like it or not? Do you realize . . .

But he had already raised his hand to strike her again.

She was wearing a bright pink scarf around her neck. She began to take it off, very slowly. Another couple was coming up the path. The man chubby and talking loudly; the woman slender and a bit stooped. She seemed to be carrying the backpack for both of them, while the man carried a notebook into which he seemed to be making notations. He nearly fell as he passed them, and they hastened, both of them, to set him aright. She looked at her husband and wanted to smile; she thought this action would amuse them both. On his part the movement was simply reflex. His anger was unabated. She gazed into his face, a face she had seen go through innumerable changes. His face changed so much! In passion it was one way; in horror, another. In joy he became flushed as a boy. In grief, his features had seemed to dissolve and a grayness crept over him.

It wasn't that she'd never seen him so angry. She'd never seen him so angry with her.

He was angry enough to kill.

The precipice to their right now seemed ominous. Far below they heard the sound of water dashing against rocks. She felt her kinship with all women who have, against their husband's will, initiated divorce. Some made it; she knew. Thousands upon thousands, and, over time, millions upon millions, did not. She said a brief prayer for them.

Do you realize, she continued, the pink scarf now held loosely in both hands, that I have done all of those things, and more, with and for you. And yet, at the moment I tell you I must have time alone to be with myself, you strike out at me. Would you call this love?

Though she was crying, she talked through the tears as if they weren't there. Her voice was calm, almost serene, though her heart was beating fast.

His face was like a storm moving in slow motion. It seemed to spread, the cloud that was his face, to cover all the space around them and then to blot out the sky. He was clenching his teeth and his hands were in fists.

She moved closer to the edge of the ledge that jutted out, creating a shallow overhang. She peered cautiously over the side.

Here, she said, pushing the scarf into his hands. You could strangle me and kick me over the edge. They wouldn't find my body for months and then it wouldn't surface near here. I'd be far downstream in no time. You'd be in the clear. I won't, she said calmly, live in fear of you.

She watched his face coalesce once more into the face she knew. He seemed to come back into himself.

You bitch, he said.

Why, because I want to be on my own?

He flung down the scarf, turned, and fled back down the trail.

When she returned to the parking lot shortly afterward he and the trusty Dodge were gone. She had trail mix in her backpack, a bottle of water, and half a box of raisins, but no money, no credit card, no driver's license. She was a hundred miles from home.

Her favorite Marlon Brando story came to her: He'd been on a talk show trying to endure it, she felt, and the host had asked him why he hadn't made it to a particular Hollywood party. Marlon said he'd tried to make it but that as he was crossing the desert his car broke down. He found himself all alone in the middle of nowhere. What did you do? asked the host, breathlessly. Well, drawled Marlon, I got out of the car, climbed on top of it, lay down, and watched the stars.

There was no time to watch the stars; she had children to get home to. But Kate realized she need not panic. She walked confidently to the edge of the parking-lot exit and held out her thumb.

When she found herself at her own door hours later, she was relieved to see the Dodge parked in its usual place. All lights in the house were out. Picking up a stone from her pretty front garden, she wrapped her pink scarf around it and carefully broke one of the panes of glass in the door. No one stirred. She let herself into the house that already felt different; it was the house of those who would remain there, not the house of the one who would leave. She could hear her husband snoring. She lay under a blanket on the couch and within minutes, her head tilted at an awkward angle, her snores became a tired, rather despondent match for his. Toward morning she felt his heavy body on top of her. He ignored her resistance. Entered her body as if he owned it. She struggled silently and at last simply ceased. She lay beneath him thinking: There's no return from this, no way we will ever come back together again. She tried to accept this clarity as a gift.

He apologized for shoving her on the trail. But never mentioned the rape. He joined a men's group. He learned men like

him allowed themselves to show only two of the so-called negative emotions, anger and fear. He'd felt them both, he said.
Anger that she wanted to leave him; fear that he wouldn't be
able to cope. She'd gazed at him and felt a wave of sickness
gathering in her heart. That she had, for years, given herself
willingly to someone who would take what she did not wish to
give; how had this happened? Within six months he'd become
lovers with his secretary, who did everything Kate had done in
the house, plus the work she did on her job. He seemed hardly
ruffled, coping.

The women could tell she was feeling better; her smile was
pensive, but there. As her body gave up the last of its bitter
memories of her first marriage, she experienced a lightness that
actually made it easier to remain seated the long hours necessary, in the boat. Now she was open, as well, to the full magic
of the journey. The shocking depth of the blue sky above their
heads, which they saw only in slivers; the cresting white of the
waves that no longer unsettled her, but which she welcomed.
Kiss the waves! the oarswomen advised. She feasted her eyes on
the darting industry of the birds, the pale dusty colors of stones
underfoot as they made camp each night; and she began to be
present to the other women whom she had largely ignored.

One night around the campfire the women were talking
about getting older, what they thought about it.

I can't bear it, said Margery, bluntly. I don't care if it's the
last bottle of hair dye in the world and a dragon is guarding it,
I'm going to get it.

I used to feel that way, said Cheryl.

I never did, said Sue.

You're kidding? they both said, looking at her. She was a
small woman with green, thoughtful eyes. It was Sue who knew

the names of plants and what their medicinal purposes might be. Sue who had said the yellow flower Kate had chewed was called desert thistleweed.

No, she said now, poking a stick into the fire and shifting on her rolled-up sleeping bag. I couldn't imagine it, even as a child. That women should do anything to their hair. I thought it was fabulous, no matter what color it was. I just couldn't fathom what was wrong with it.

She laughed.

What was wrong with it, said Margery, was that it started turning white!

Gray, said Cheryl. Gray had such terrible associations, I used to think. It was the color of blandness, dullness. Lifelessness. But then I began to notice stones and water, and gray skies, not to complain about but to appreciate. If you've ever lived through a drought you appreciate gray skies. Rain. Rain is gray, she said.

Her hair was long and silvery white; she wore it in a ponytail while they were on the boat; now it hung free and the moonlight rested lovingly on it. The beauty of it there in the canyon, where every boulder, tree, and bush held its natural color, could not be denied.

Kate laughed, and the women turned to her.

I always tell people I am too absentminded to remember to color my hair, she said, but the truth is, I am too vain.

The women waited for more.

Oh, I tried it for a while. And actually got to be fairly good at it. I was never of the color every strand every single month school. I was more of the color it every couple of months, who cares about trying to do it perfectly.

They laughed, partly at Kate's animation. She'd been too sick to join in their talks before.

But then, she continued, I began to experience a feeling I hadn't felt since high school, when I first began straightening my hair. I began to feel humiliated. It felt like I was abusing myself. Hiding something important that was not really at fault. Besides, I started to feel I was missing what was going on with me. The incredible change; it had to mean something. What did it mean? I wondered.

She leaned back on her sleeping bag, and looked around at the women in her circle. There were five of them. Another circle of four sat and sprawled around a smaller fire a few yards away. It felt luxurious to be out camping with a band of mature women, and Kate reveled in the intimacy engendered by their distance from everything and everyone they knew.

I used to straighten my hair, in the sixties, said Lauren. She had short, bright red hair that curled around her ears. It was long then, *very*, and I straightened it with an electric iron. *On an ironing board*. I was quite the contortionist.

The women laughed to think of the fads of youth.

Kate remembered sitting in the beauty shop, which never, in those days, seemed clean and bright enough, and watching the women undergo the torture of having their hair straightened with hot combs. It had not occurred to her to question this behavior at the time: What could be so wrong with our natural hair? And then of course, at college there had been chemical "relaxers." Painless, unless the cosmetologist poured on too much, or mixed it too strong. She'd dreaded going to the shop, and never understood how other young girls enjoyed it. They seemed to suffer willingly, or, more likely, now that she thought of it, they had probably ignored the process. Choosing to focus on the results. She remembered all of them sitting listlessly, oblivious to self-danger, heads in magazines, waiting their turn.

Sometimes now she colored her hair, just for fun. But she

never did it in the spirit of covering up her age. Her recognition of such an entrenched vanity eventually amused her.

I'm glad of the tucks and sucks too, said Margery. I've had both. And.

Tell us, said Sue.

And so it continued until bedtime. One story leading to another, no woman's story more important than another's. Every woman's choices honored as her own.

The tenth night on the river she dreamed of her mother. Her body mangled by the car crash. Her head however completely unmarked, her eyes and face clear. When Kate looked down at her hands, she saw one of them was missing. The other was busy untangling what looked like a fishing net. They were sitting beside the ocean, and her mother gazed out upon it as she spoke: *It puzzled me that you did not understand,* she said.

But how could I understand? Kate asked. *I was never told* anything.

The secret is, you do not have to be told, said her mother, finishing the net, and now holding it with two whole hands, preparing to fling it into the sea. *We do not need a boat for this,* she added, anticipating Kate's question.

Kate woke up and lay in her sleeping bag watching the dawn. She could hear the oarswomen readying their boats. Soon it would be time to pack up her gear and stuff it in the waterproof duffel folded neatly beside a nearby tree.

Her mother's face, patient and wise, came back to her, as it had appeared in the dream. How beautiful her mother had been! A sunny brown, with thick black hair, compassionate but shrewdly intelligent eyes that missed very little, and a readiness to make and laugh at jokes that had endeared her to everyone

who knew her. Kate's father had adored her since they were
both six years old.

Her hand had grown back, she fished without a boat. Why
did she even need the net? thought Kate.

All day in the little dorie Kate thought about the dream. For
that one enigmatic moment with her mother, she would have
made the river journey. Though she had brought nothing to
write on, she knew she must begin a story about a mother and a
daughter. Borrowing a tiny Post-it pad from Avoa, who loved
dreams, both having them herself and hearing and interpreting
those of other people, she began.

*It was a sultry summer day, the day we buried my mother.
The night before, at the wake, I stood over her body and tried
to peer straight into her brain. She was shrunken from the cancer she'd battled the last years of her life; her mouth was twisted
from the suffering she had endured. The flowers arrayed around
her coffin smelled heavy and wet. I felt desperate for fresh air.
Why were you so dissatisfied with me? I asked her.*

*In the kitchen my younger sister embraced me. We had not
seen each other in nearly a decade. Unlike me, she was slender
and dark. Her hair now streaked with silver. My older sister, her
hair a russet that matched her dress, and her shoes, was busy
making potato salad, her specialty. My father sat at the kitchen
table nursing a cup of chamomile tea.*

*"Daddy, you must eat something." It seemed to me Tonya
was always saying something like this. She was a natural-born
comforter. I couldn't have imagined a wake without her in
charge of it.*

*Now she stood over our father, as our mother might have;
her arm around his shoulders. They looked very much alike.
Firm-fleshed (even though Dad looked really old) and dark, with*

eyes that lit up their faces. They shared an easily aroused animation and love of good times.

He nodded at his cup.

"That's nothing," she said. "Tea. Have some chicken. Potato salad."

"I can't eat," he said. He tilted his head in the direction of the living room.

"She would want you to," said Tonya.

Harriet gave me an absentminded shove toward the food.

"You eat something too, Roberta."

I was named for my father.

"Daddy," I said, taking the hand that now clung to the teacup, "you and I are going to have some dinner." He grunted.

"No refusals and no hesitation allowed."

"Oh, well," he said, looking up.

My father adored me. He thought I was just right. Though named for him, I didn't look like him at all.

I took two plates from the pile on the table, and moved toward the pots on the stove. I sensed rather than saw the dejection in the faces of both my sisters. I had always been able to wrap our father around my finger. He'd always listened to me.

"Um," I said, forking up collard greens.

"I knew Roberta would get you to eat," said Tonya, who'd cooked all the food.

Harriet said nothing. The hug between us now felt forgotten.

This was as much as Kate could write on the Post-its. She stuffed the story in her duffel along with her hiking boots and toiletries, and settled herself comfortably in the boat. Overhead there were vultures and crows, black and graceful against the terra cotta canyon walls. She daydreamed about the drift of her

life; the lover in her house, in her bed. The recurring dream of
the dry river. Her therapist's skepticism that she knew what she
was doing, going out to run a live river in her waking life.

She felt no stirring within. Though perhaps her mother's
visit had been one. It had been a very long time since she'd
dreamed of her. After the crash, after identifying the bodies,
she'd feared nightmares, but she'd been spared those. Her poor
father's body had been crushed like an accordion. She shud-
dered now to remember it. And yet, she felt she must remember
it, linger over her response to it, there under the open protection
of the sky, in the middle of charging waters, vulnerable to being dashed against rocks herself. She had longed to touch some
whole part of him. And found that whole part in one of his feet.
She'd grasped his toes, so long and hairy on their tops, and
she'd caressed them until she felt satisfied. They never warmed
from her hands, not the slightest bit. That was what being dead
meant, she thought.

Now she realized that she was weeping, just a little, and that
a pain in her shoulder, carried so long she'd gotten used to it,
seemed to be shifting closer to the surface of her skin. She began
to rotate her shoulders. Avoa, sitting next to her, began to rotate
hers as well. Before long they were doing miniaturized yoga
postures in the tiny boat.

Ahead of them the other women's boat was entering unusually powerful rapids. As they watched, startled, it overturned.
They had barely time to think before they were running the
same rapids. She wondered if they too would be flung into the
river. But no, their oarswoman steered them slightly more to
the left of a huge boulder that rose up like an iceberg in the middle of the river. They sped past the others, all swimming madly
toward the shore.

That night, as they sat around the campfire, she was flooded with gratitude. To see the women safe, to hear their humorous stories of their surprise, their fright. To know they had depended on their own strength and courage to pull themselves to shore.

That night, in the adrenaline glow of having survived, the talk was, of course, about sex.

How much and how often, right? said Margery, drying her hair with a towel and throwing a fistful of dried twigs on the fire.

How long and how much does size matter, anyway? said Cheryl, biting into a chocolate bar she'd stashed for just such an occasion.

The women laughed.

"Gimme something that's not hard,/Come on, come on."

Sue sang the refrain from John Lennon and Yoko Ono's "Give Me Something," from their *Double Fantasy* album. She loved Ono for recording what sounded like a live orgasm.

There's a period in there where you really don't want anything hard, said Kate.

Not me, said Cheryl. I fantasize big, hard, and long.

And black? asked Kate.

Cheryl colored. Sometimes, yes, she said. I'll never forget the day I ambled into Good Vibrations and there it was, hanging on the wall.

The women roared.

There's fantasy and then there's, ah, actual flesh, said Annie, an oarswoman their own age, who had come over to join them. Firm is one thing; hard is something else, she said. She was a wiry Texan with a hawk's nose and piercing gray eyes. Her wild white-streaked hair fanned out around her faded red baseball cap. The young can handle hard, she said; at our age firm is very acceptable. She lay back and looked thoughtfully into the fire. I once had a lover who preferred the term *full*. He thought being hard inside me would be painful, and it was.

Nature takes care of it very well, said Margery. If only someone would tell men it's okay. Not to be hard as a rock, not to need to drive a woman through the bed.

Sally, wandering over from the other campfire, overheard this comment.

Well, she said, laughing with the women, I can see where the inquiring mind needs to be.

Oh, yes, said Cheryl, come sit with the big girls. We'll tell you what time of night it is.

I can't believe you're all straight, said Sue.

There was a long pause.

I've been straight for incredibly long periods, said Margery. Thoughtfully.

The women hooted.

The moon overhead was creamy and round. The river was a wide yellow thread through the canyon. No longer on it, the women felt their kinship still. It was as if it now moved through their bodies, even while they slept.

She was drawn to Sue. She seemed so plain, so clear, so unadorned. They had separated from the others and were exploring caves, and their petroglyphs, high above the canyon floor.

I have always lived with women, said Sue, from the very beginning.

Didn't you miss having a boyfriend? asked Kate.

Why would I miss what I never had? asked Sue, studying the triumphant figure of a woman giving birth. It was almost shocking, the power expressed in the woman's attitude. The rock the artist had chosen was tall and round, like a person with its belly protruding. The woman giving birth was carved on the belly.

Amazing, that artists were so alike, throughout eons. As giving birth was the same. But not the ecstatic sense of a woman's power. That had changed, drastically. Now most women actually thought the doctor delivered the baby. Amazing.

Kate was silent, thinking of how she'd begun missing having a boyfriend long before having one. A boyfriend had seemed inevitable. The older girls at school talked about boys all the time, and had boyfriends. Her parents were there in front of her every single day; her mother cherishing, her father positively doting. It had seemed so natural. The only way to go. Her girl friends at school had certainly never appealed to her. They seemed too much like her, always worrying about how they looked, what to wear, how their hair was doing. She liked to go shopping with them, liked to eat and study with them. The thought of kissing one of them had never crossed her mind. In fact, even now, the thought of kissing one of *them* made her queasy.

Boys never interested me, said Sue. I always got along well with them, but nary a romantic thought had I. Now, though, I'm celibate.

Really, said Kate. Her hand rested near a carving of a large sunburst. A tiny figure that looked like a goat raised its head as if enjoying the radiance. She had never expected to find signs of human life in the canyons that radiated out from the main one. At a place far from the river that was reached after a long climb that began behind a waterfall they'd come to the place the Hopi claimed as the spot they'd emerged into the present world. The fourth world. The worlds before that had been destroyed. And at that spot, there had been a human handprint. She had felt the impact of that small handprint as if it were a handshake. Someone from centuries, perhaps thousands of years, past, reaching out to her. It was in a very awkward place, impossible to touch, and so she had blown a kiss of thanks. And bowed deeply.

Thank you, artist, she had said. You are our help when we can receive no other.

At first, said Sue, I thought I was different because my mother did not love me. Was I always looking for a loving mother? This was the question put to me by countless shrinks. I kinda didn't think so. She grinned. After all, I found so many of them. You'd think I'd eventually have had enough.

Enough? asked Kate.

Loving mothers, said Sue.

I find I don't really have a preference, said Kate.

Really, said Sue.

People are remarkably similar, said Kate, when you relate to individuals. What do I like, she mused, as they sat on a boulder in the sun. Well, passion and gentleness and good humor and . . .

I suppose some men have that, said Sue. I'm still not interested.

Kate laughed.

What a time they lived in, she thought. At least those of us living in the West, in the present century, instead of in the Middle East or other parts of the world where time, for women, had stopped in the Middle Ages. There were women on the planet who were not allowed to show their faces. Not permitted to smile at a man who was not a relative without the possibility of being beaten. There were women being stoned, for showing legs or hair. And yet, the carvings all around them spoke of another time before the present and before, even, the recorded past. A time when women were joyous about their naked bodies. Free.

She thought of the bumper sticker that some wily feminist had created: DON'T DIE WONDERING. And she wouldn't. She'd found pleasure eventually in relating to women as lovers. But she couldn't claim she thought they were better, as lovers, or as partners, than men. And this was, actually, a great comfort to her; she felt, finally, in emotional and erotic balance. Having parents whom she loved fairly equally, she'd been puzzled on some level that she must, as an adult, choose to relate primarily to one or the other sex. Whose idea was this, really? she wondered. Freud's? And what a lot of lies he'd told trying to avoid facing his own childhood sex abuse. Because of him generations of people had believed three-year-olds knowingly seduced their grandfathers! She had accepted the adventures before her, and had, so far, survived them. And now, like the artists of old, carving their knowledge of ecstasy and power on rocks, she could leave a gentle, indelible message of self-love to all humans everywhere.

And now, perhaps it was time to leave that area of exploration, and, like Sue, to enter another: the life of the virgin, one who is whole unto herself.

So that is how you have changed, he said to her, when she returned. That is the one change I would never have guessed!

They were lying cozily in bed, her leg over his. In the old days this position itself would have been an invitation.

Are you sure? he asked.

It isn't, as it must seem, a mental decision, she said.

He waited.

And I don't think it's forever. But what do I know?

Please don't be too angry with me, he said. But I'm not ready. Would you consider tapering off gradually? I'm not ready to lose this part of our life yet.

She lay, only a moment, reflecting.

I'm not ready either, I think.

He grinned.

Oh, don't be so cocky, she said.

Making love, tapering off, was a way of being gentle to them both.

And now when she lay in his arms she savored and grieved the richness, the sweetness, the sharp edge of intimacy she would be leaving. She felt she would be leaving the body itself. But there was a land beyond the sexual body, and friends like Sue proved it. They were out there in it, already, inhabiting new forests, sailing new seas.

And Sure Enough

AND SURE ENOUGH, ALMOST THE FIRST WORDS out of the shaman's mouth were: no sex. He was short and brown and round with an open and friendly face. *Young.* She was surprised. She'd thought shamans had to be old, thin, a bit haggard by their wisdom. A trifle gloomy. But no, Armando Juarez was in his forties, and, though he had grandchildren, he seemed as jolly and nimble as a boy. His straight black hair was cut just below his ears, his black eyes gazed merrily back at the group. They were seven. Five women, ages forty to sixty-five; two men, a slender New Yorker of a youthful, ambiguous age and an older man, perhaps forty-five, from Utah.

Not with yourself, he joked. And not with each other.

Could we ask why? asked Kate.

Maybe the medicine is jealous, said the man from Utah, chuckling.

Armando was serious. It is because that is how it is, he said. From time before time. Making love is something we enjoy, of course. But it has its place and time that is not the same place and time as the Grandmother medicine. This medicine, you will see, is from the Grandmother. That is its spirit. Grandmothers are not sexy.

That's what you think, muttered one of the women, and everyone smiled. Including Armando.

You're right, that's not the reason, he said. Don't tell my wife I said something so stupid. She would kill me.

There was a long silence.

It is to pay respect, he said finally, reflectively. It is to have an experience of the soul that is undistracted by desire.

Oh me, oh my, said the youngish New Yorker.

Kate had met this group at the airport only hours before. It was the first time any of them had visited this country. The first time any of them had traveled to South America. At the airport they'd recognized one another immediately as Medicine Seekers. There they stood, speaking only a halting, basic Spanish, those who spoke it at all. Loaded down with backpacks, baseball caps and straw hats, waterproof duffels, sturdy sandals or boots.

They had the look of people deliberately distancing themselves from the center of things, as their own cultures defined it. Seeking the edge, the fringe. But also, paradoxically, the heart. At least they hoped so.

Again Kate found herself in a tiny boat, thousands of miles from anyone she knew, on a river, the Amazon this time, heading for the forest.

He had watched her go. This time, because he was going somewhere too, they'd parted at the airport at home. He'd carried her brown duffel and her faded mauve backpack, and she'd carried her bag of oranges. They stood at the back of the line as people boarded the plane, their bundles around their feet, their bodies touching. At last it was time for her to board. He hugged her, she raised herself a bit, they kissed.

Enjoy Hawaii, she said. I almost wish I were going with you.

Somewhere safe: mellow people, danceable music, beautiful girls.

He laughed. No, you don't, he said.

I don't even know why I'm going the other way, she said, with a mock grimace, as the flight attendant took her ticket.

You have to, he said.

Who knew! she said, shrugging, disappearing toward the plane.

Apparently enlightenment of any sort required a lot of regurgitation. Kate remembered telling a friend about her experience with magic mushrooms. How much they'd helped her when she'd been overwhelmed with grief. It had been a time in the seventies when she finally got it that the earth was being destroyed; that human beings were living in a time when Time was running out. She'd taken the medicine with no idea it would help her. It had appeared seemingly out of nowhere, an odd visitor had brought it. Really she'd taken it because she didn't care anymore. Any reality seemed better than the one she was in. That of knowing humans had fouled their nest so badly it would no longer nurture them. And the first thing that happened was she'd gotten rotten sick. Nausea. Worse than being pregnant. And she'd thrown up.

She'd urged her friend to try the medicine. But the friend dismissed it. I can't bear being nauseous, she'd said.

But there's the other side of being nauseous, Kate said. You get to the other side. And that is where you want to get. It's not just about being sick to your gills.

No, thanks, said the friend. I couldn't do it.

Kate thought of this as she sat, shivering, hunched over a hole that had been dug in front of her in the ground.

They'd been asked to drink half a gallon of a frothy liquid

that tasted like soapsuds. This was to provoke the vomiting and the diarrhea that would clean them out. You could never put a sacred medicine into a polluted body. The heavy meat eaters, if there were any, were especially warned. Fortunately, for this trip, unlike all the others in her life, she'd read everything she could find on what this experience with plant medicines might be. She'd even gone to a local shaman at home, surprised that one lived within driving distance of her. What was happening in the world, she had wondered, that it was possible to call up a shaman who spoke your language and whose voice mail said yes, call again, there might be a space for you? She had gone, taken the horrible-tasting medicine, and for the next seven hours, after the gut-wrenching nausea and diarrhea, had sat wearing a black mask over her eyes, and watched the pictures her plant friends drew for her. It was exactly like being in school, but with fascinating text material. The teacher however was unique. She was Grandmother. The oldest Being who ever lived. Her essence that of Primordial Female Human Being As Tree. Surprisingly, she was not angry. Or even, apparently, perturbed. It was as if she were explaining how a pet project she'd personally sponsored had somehow gone wrong. But this was only the tiniest part of it.

The waves of nausea were like real waves, bending her double by their force. Into the hole went everything that wasn't internally attached. And though the waves were powerful, her dislike of them was not. This was different; even vomiting so violently that her body was bathed in sweat, Kate noticed this. She saw that even though throwing up is itself revolting, she had, after many sessions with Grandmother, learned to do it well; almost elegantly. She smiled, even as another wave rocked her off her rough-hewn log seat and to her shaken knees. She did not care anymore about the discomfort of this phase. She knew a phase was all it was. That beyond this three hours of drinking soapsuds and vomiting and going to the bushes, Grandmother waited, just as she had waited for indigenous people sick with disease and fear for thousands of years.

I am an American, Kate thought. Indigenous to the Americas. Nowhere else could I, this so-called Black person—African, European, Indio—exist. Only here. In Africa there would have been no Europeans, no Native Americans. In Europe, no Africans and no Indians. Only here; *only here,* she said, as the waves of vomiting continued past the three hours and into the evening. I will bear this as long as it takes. This old medicine surely must care for, belong to, me.

She was grateful when Armando brought a new drink, pinkish, and lifted it to her lips. It calmed her stomach immediately. He gave her water. For dinner that night, the last meal they would have for fourteen days, he boiled fish from the river and gave them its broth.

She had read many books about the rainforest, and had longed to meet it. She thought like this. That whenever you go someplace, you meet it, as if it were alive, which of course it is. Now she rested in her hut a few steps from the river and listened to this Being, the rainforest. Why had she ever thought it would be silent? It was the loudest thing she'd ever heard. Like trains and planes and the New York City subway at rush hour. It was so loud, in fact, it actually did remind her of New York. And she thought about the aptness of calling the city "the jungle." Little did they know! Or perhaps they did. And every sound she heard that was not made by the vegetation, giant trees and tree-sized vines, groaning as they rubbed against one another, was made by creatures. Every Being was chatting, talking, whistling, singing. *Singing.* Lots of that. And everything was in motion. If she listened closely she could distinguish slithering, sliding, jump-

ing, hopping, ambling, crawling, flying. The cry of a jaguar sent
a ripple of fear through their little camp; she could feel it, even
though their huts were spread out in the forest, out of sight of
one another. It was so loud and offered with such proprietary
authority she knew it would make most of them want to run.
She thought about running, but where would she go? After
a hot and dusty four hours to the river, in a grime-encrusted
Toyota that seemed older than Japanese culture, it had taken
them half a day on the river, to push off, paddle, and motor to
the camp. The boat, an ancient dugout with a rusty outboard
motor, had deposited them and left. The boatman promised to
return in two weeks. The river was full of crocodiles and piranha.
She watched the crocodiles slithering from river bank to river all
along their route; though she'd read piranha ate you up only if
you were already bleeding. Just her luck she'd tripped on a rock,
in the seconds between changing boots for sandals to wear
around the camp, and cut her big toe. Kate rummaged around
beneath her mosquito net for her night bag. Finding it, she ex-
tracted crimson earplugs.

Yolo

YOLO? ASKED THE DESK CLERK? THAT'S A NAME?
You betcha, said Yolo. And the other part of it is Day.

He thought, surely living in Hawaii with all these weird Hawaiian names for everything, including people, haoles should have no trouble with something as short and sweet as Yolo.

The guy was wearing one of those shirts every haole who goes to Hawaii buys at the airport. Red with white hibiscus flowers. His blond hair, very pale skin, and eyes just did not look Hawaiian. But Yolo decided not to be critical. He'd come to Hawaii on one of those cheap flights the average working artist can afford, and it had come with this hotel, which did sit, miraculously, right at the edge of the sea. It was ugly, the hotel, the same beige of office buildings in Washington, D.C., but sitting by the water his back would be to it.

He missed his old lady. He imagined her stoned out of her mind, hanging in a hammock in a jungle so far away he couldn't even imagine it. Why do some people put themselves through it! he thought. Stumped by her persistence.

Up in his room, which faced the beach, he stripped. Throwing off his mainland clothes as if they were infested with lice.

Instead of unpacking he simply dumped everything from his suitcase onto the floor. There in the pile was his new palm-green bathing suit. He put it on, facing the mirror that reflected the entire room, and grinned to see how trim and, well, cute he was. He had Frederick Douglass kind of hair, wiry and energetic, and looked a bit like him, because his ancestry was the same: His mother was mostly Anglo-Indian, his father mostly African. This mixture gave you really good skin, he thought, vainly admiring his own, and medium bushy hair that was actually manageable. His hair was long and, released from the braids he usually wore it in, hung nicely down his back. Some of the other mixtures could cause a couple of bad hair days. He smiled, looking for his suntan lotion. Not suntan. He always forgot. *Sunblock*. Horrible, that now humans had to block the rays of the sun. But hey, with his mixture, he got a whopping dose of natural sunblock, from his dad: Thank you, Mother Africa! While from his mom, not to leave out her European contributions, he got a nice reflective quality. He imagined the too strong sun rays bouncing off the mica of her white genes. All things considered, he didn't expect to suffer from skin cancer.

His mind was like this. Running on a lot of the time about himself. He tried to hide this sometimes from Kate, but she only laughed. Most people are like that, she said. We are our most interesting subject. When we're free to think about ourselves, not about the kids, not about the car, house, or payments on our various purchases, and not about our work, well, guess what? We natter on about ourselves.

They were both vain. And what do we have to be vain about? they sometimes asked themselves. We're considered second- and third-class citizens of a country whose government never wanted us. Except as slaves. We understand by now the world will be blown to bits, doubtless by this same government, before people of color get their fair share. We can't afford health insurance, nor will it even ever be applicable, the way things are going. Nobody but us wants to be Black. And yet, we're vain.

We like our stubbornness, Yolo had offered.

Our contrariness, said Kate. We never want to do anything the way they do it. We think that of any two choices given they are likely to pick the most boring one.

We like being brown, Yolo said, nose-kissing her under-arm. A choice they could have made easily except it frightened them. What did they do with the brown offspring they had? They sold them. What a message to send your kids, of whatever color.

And yet, "sold down the river," his great-great-grandparents and their parents before them had somehow survived. Though how they'd managed to live without their mothers he simply could not understand. As old as he was the thought of losing his mother, for any reason, including old age and readiness, made him want to cry. Africans were said to be the most attached to their children of all peoples the Europeans encountered. You could make the mother especially do anything by threatening to harm her child.

And our unique hair, said Kate. Do you realize everybody else's hair, on the entire planet, is straight?

Well, compared to ours, he'd said, laughing and kissing her graying locks.

At last he was blissed out on the beach, *The Mists of Avalon* in one hand, a gin and tonic in the other. Kate had given him an-other book to read called *Shark Dialogues,* a book about, as she put it, The Real Hawaii, but he had left it in his room. The sea was azure enough to make you weep. He was in paradise. If only his woman was with him and not off in some jungle probably by now trying to communicate with a snake.

In this relaxed, bemused frame of mind, he dozed.

Hey, bradda!

Slowly and reluctantly opening his eyes he saw a very large man. Brown with a protruding belly. Dark eyes and long wavy hair. He was wearing frayed denim cutoffs and that was all. He looked like . . . Damn, he looked like something Yolo had not seen since coming to Hawaii. He looked like maybe a Hawaiian.

Hey, bradda man, for want you come oba deah. The man was pointing.

What was he speaking? Yolo dragged himself out of the land of gin and pleasant dreams and squinted toward the end of the beach where the man was pointing. He could see nothing.

What is it? he asked. What can I do for you?

The man seemed surprised.

Oh, he said. I thought . . .

Yolo was on his feet. Grabbing his straw hat and quickly shoving his feet into sandals because the sand was fiercely hot.

I'm sorry, said the man, I thought you was a bradda.

I am, actually, said Yolo.

There was silence. The man looked toward the hotel, considered something for a moment. Turned back to Yolo and said, If you don't mind. I'm very sorry. But I need to ask you to do something. It will take only a little while. I have to go home and get something and I need to ask you to stay with something I need to leave protected on the beach.

Oh shit, thought Yolo.

Are you a fisherman? he asked.

Yes, said the man. I was fishing.

Yolo thought of being asked to guard a boatload of mari-juana. He wanted to say no. He wanted to explain about his va-cation. How much he needed one. How much he deserved one. He'd painted furiously all year and had made just enough to pay his bills, keep the heat going, and have this vacation!

On the other hand, he was trying to have a vacation where someone else was working. He thought: What would *she* do? He stepped back a bit from the man. Looked him up and down. He noticed his eyes were sad and a bit bloodshot. His hair blown every which way. Still, it was what his father would call "a good face." Nothing menacing or malignant seemed to have ever inhabited it. He hadn't missed any meals in his life either, which said something about his stability.

Let's go, he said.

Down the beach they walked, the big man, who said his name was Jerry SomethingVeryComplicated, (Izkamakawiwo'ole!), lead-ing the way. The beach was longer than it looked from where he'd lain in his incredibly comfy beach lounger. There was a narrow, shallow river emptying into the ocean that they needed to cross. On the other side of the river there were no chairs, no umbrellas. The place seemed still wild.

This part of the beach for da locals, said Jerry, as if to ex-plain.

Does that mean you can't go to the beach on the hotel side? asked Yolo.

Who can afford it? said Jerry, shrugging.

The beach made a curious turn to the left, around some black, deeply pitted lava rocks. Out of sight of the hotel there was anchored a small, battered fishing boat. They walked toward it. As they came closer to it and because he was looking

at the boat and not at the ground, Yolo almost stumbled over a
young man lying on the sand. He seemed so peaceful, napping
there in the sun, that Yolo could not believe he was dead.

The shock on his face must have been apparent.

He dead, bradda, yeah, said Jerry.

The Curious Thing

THE CURIOUS THING ABOUT THE GRANDMOTHER medicine was that people would take it, even though it tasted ghastly. Even more curious was that it continued to taste horrible, in fact more and more horrible the longer you took it. By now Kate could feel the muscles of her throat contract just thinking about it. If she actually saw it in the shaman's bottle, she wanted to vomit. Armando laughed at them each time he called them to circle. They all came looking pitiful, he teased them, like goats going to the butcher. He pretended to be unmoved by the disgusting flavor of the medicine, and drank some each time they journeyed. Tonight Kate sat facing the river, which splashed lazily down below their palapa.

She was feeling weak from the continuous internal cleansing of the day before. Everyone else also seemed pale and less than steady on their feet. It was extremely hot; even so, because of parasites living in the sand and poisonous snakes and who knows what all, they were required to wear tall rubber boots most of the time. Entering the large ceremonial palapa they removed their boots and left them outside. Everyone stretched their bodies, settling into their respective seats, and wriggled and massaged their toes.

When it was her turn to take the medicine, she asked, as she always did, for help for the humans of the planet and for the coming generations and for the animals and plants and rocks. She asked that she be guided to knowledge of how to act in the world for the highest good of all. She asked that the medicine accept her and do no harm. She called on the Grandmother Spirit to protect her, while she was being taught. With a tightening of her throat, which she consciously acknowledged and willfully relaxed, she drank the medicine in a gulp. Even so, she gagged. What was its flavor? Worse than any kind of excrement, surely, she thought.

And people had willingly taken this medicine for thousands of years! Repugnant as it was. How could she not love these people? After everyone, including Armando, had taken the medicine, there was a languid, hazy interlude. A feeling of: It is done. Whatever happens now, there will be no turning back. She particularly appreciated this time; it was like being in a small boat, all together, and knowing you would travel the length of the river together and hopefully reach your destination and with good fortune land in a place that welcomed you.

The New Yorker was the first to head for the bushes. Rushing out without his boots or his flip-flops, which lay beside the entrance. Soon they could hear him vomiting. That triggered one of the women, who went out, slowly, calmly, carefully bending over to place her flip-flops on her feet. Next, the man from Utah, his tall body slightly stooping going out the low entrance, his head brushing the palm fronds that formed the palapa's top. And then the rest of them, one by one, left the circle. Some went to their holes and leaned over them. Others wandered out into the forest. She went to the forest. Found a tree that looked like an ancient woman, her head in the heavens, her feet in the earth, and, touching it lightly to ask permission, she threw up whatever poisons might be left in her body.

Returning, she noticed the light had changed. It was now late afternoon. They would be sitting for at least four hours before the mosquitoes began their nightly hunt. But this did not concern her very much, though she was allergic to insect bites and was already swollen from them. She had no mirror but she felt her eyes were almost swollen shut. She closed them.

The first time she had gone to visit Grandmother she had been fleeing the frightened animal aspect of herself. It seemed to her that humans were now in the position of deer or antelope or buffalo or polar bears. There wasn't any longer a safe place for any of them. And yet she hated being afraid because fear was so paralyzing. She knew that if human beings, on a global level, gave in to the fear of being wiped out, disposable, like all the other creatures, they would never be able to think and feel their way out of their dilemma.

And so she had sat in a car crossing a long silver bridge, holding a new friend's hand. This was a woman who seemed to be exactly where she was. In a state of near catatonic panic. Let's go ask the trees! this woman had said, the first time Kate looked her in the eye and said: Hi, what's happening?

Had He Been Shot?

HAD HE BEEN SHOT, STRANGLED, OR DROWNED? There was no way of telling, from looking at the body. Yolo sat close to it, just where the warm moist sand met the hotter dry sand, and where apparently the body had washed up. There was no blood. He saw no puncture wound. No rope burn around the young man's neck. He wanted to touch him. Cautiously, looking all about, up and down the deserted beach, he leaned over and lifted gently a strand of brownish-black hair that blew across the peaceful face. He had a feeling of fatherhood. Maybe even grandfatherhood. The boy was so young. So incredibly good-looking, wearing only threadbare shorts, a string of blue beads around his neck, and a silver ring in his right ear. Whatever troubles he'd faced in life were forgotten now, as Yolo wished they might have been while he was still alive.

He felt very present, waiting there beside the body. Present and useful. Drawing his legs up he sat in the lotus position and began to meditate. After half an hour he stirred, stretched his legs, and began to wonder if he were being tricked. But no, looking behind him toward "da locals' " parking lot, which was unpaved and partly obscured by scraggly trees, he saw Jerry returning with what looked like a troop, all of them walking heavily, their heads down, as if resigned to receiving bad news.

Jerry introduced him with a nod and briefly explained why he was there. Yolo stepped back immediately, outside the circle of the men.

He did not leave, however. Later, he would wonder why he did not. He stood watching their expressions as each of the men looked at the body of the young man. On some faces there were tears. One of the men, an older version of the dead man, went swiftly to his knees and held the body in his arms. He was smoking a cigarette and Yolo thought how odd it was, how rarely seen, this scene: a living brother holding a dead one with cigarette smoke curling in the air behind them.

Working in silence two of the men wrapped the body in a tattered bedspread and hoisted it onto their shoulders. Yolo followed them to the parking lot and over to a battered pea-green van. After carefully laying the body inside, the men shut the door.

He stayed a long time in the parking lot, looking at the bare earth, the footprints, the occasional gum wrapper and beer can. Then he looked out to sea. Seeing the ocean reminded him of his vacation. He started back toward the hotel, back toward his lounge chair, his novel. But he doubted he could really return to any of it.

When Kate Had Visited

WHEN KATE HAD VISITED A LOCAL SHAMAN, AN African-Amerindian woman who had studied with Armando years before, she had been charmed, before completely going under, by Armando's voice as he sang *icaros,* healing songs that had come down to him through countless generations, which Anunu had on tape. *Ya es el tiempo para abrir tu corazón.* Now is the time to open your heart. This was the line that she always understood, no matter how distracted or apprehensive she was at the beginning of the journey. It never failed to make her feel the rightness of her decision to be where she was. Sitting in the dark, drinking a horrible-tasting mixture of an unseen, unknown tree and vine from another continent, and being totally dependent on a woman who was as unknown as either tree or vine. Anunu was small and dark and ageless with shrewd bright eyes that asked nothing of you except that you be willing to approach her as yourself. This was a lot, of course, and many people could not do it.

Grandmother will want to know all about you, she smiled, and She will find out, too. She laughed. You might as well tell me a little bit of what brought you here today so that I will be better able to help you on your journey.

Kate had not hesitated.

I believe all is up with us, she said. Us humans.

And whatever would make you believe that? asked Anunu, with a chuckle.

Kate laughed as well.

It's all so fucked, she said. She was surprised she had used this term. Ordinarily she was more mindful in her speech. She had reasoned it wrong to use *fuck* as a curse, for instance. If *fucking* is used as a curse, she believed, soon the act of fucking, which she considered healthy and succulent, would cause its participants to self-destruct. AIDS did not surprise her, at this level of thought, because it had seemed to crawl out of the global human shadow bag into which sex had been consigned.

I am also unconvinced of the need to do anything further with my life, she said.

Anunu was silent, looking at her intently.

It is such a fine life, said Anunu.

Kate was surprised. Although she was widely published and was to some extent a public figure, she had the idea most of the time that she was unrecognizable and therefore incognito. This grew out of her feeling when she was a child that she had the power to be invisible, which grew out of the fact that frequently she had felt unseen.

And, said Kate into Anunu's silence, there is the question of sex. One's sexuality.

Ah, said Anunu.

I don't seem to find much of a difference between women and men when it comes to loving them. If they're wonderful, sexy, and cute, I want to snuggle up and be enchanted.

They both laughed.

Well, said Anunu. That's not a problem. The other two might be, but that's not.

I don't think so either, said Kate. I don't understand why people have such a hard time seeing it's impossible to be only one thing; and to love only one gender or one race. At least it seems impossible for me. It would be like thinking only beautiful people have green eyes. Limitation is willful and childish, she said. And so much less fun.

It's not that interesting, no, said Anunu. But it's been an excellent way, for thousands of years, to keep a society's labor force under control.

Kate nodded. Her brain began to perk up more, to start to click with thought, the way it did when she met someone she could talk "shorthand" with. Talking with Anunu she thought maybe she didn't need to take the Ayahuasca. Otherwise known as yagé. Grandmother.

Anunu was speaking softly, looking into Kate's face with such kindness!

Oh, she said, what I've discovered is that with lovers as with everything, there are cycles, seasons. If you live your life in such a way as to become free rather than to become not free, she continued, you will find Life presents you with regular summers and winters and autumns and springs. There will be times when the masculine will demand your interest and attention, she said. Times when the feminine will rise and exact her due.

She sat back in her orange-sunset-colored chair and interlaced her long fingers. For instance, she said, when I began to hear Grandmother calling me, I noticed more and more men coming into my life. It is all Grandmother, of course, she said, chuckling, *regardless of appearances!* As they say in the Church of Religious Science about God. And there were all these men— can you guess why?

Kate shook her head. Uh-uh, she said, I hope they were cute.

Some were, said Anunu. Some were definitely not. She laughed. But to a man they were ethnobotanists.

Ethno-whats? asked Kate.

Folks who study people's relationships with their plants. That is, the plants that grow around them.

Kate leaned forward in her seat. She felt like a gong had gone off in her head. *Bong.* This always happened when a single word triggered awareness that she had stumbled onto the right path. *People and their plants. Plants and their people.* She had an instinctive understanding, perhaps from birth, that people and plants were relatives. As a child she had spent hours talking to, caressing, sitting in, kissing, and otherwise trying to communicate with trees. As a very young child she'd been convinced that trees had mouths and that she could find a mouth on a tree if only she grew tall enough and looked for it very hard.

Why can't they talk? she'd once asked her mother, who'd laughed and told everyone about the funny question her little daughter had asked.

It was clear she had met an inspirer in Anunu and that they could continue talking well into the afternoon. Her friend was sitting outside the door, however, waiting for her own interview.

Later, back in the room in which they were to work, Anunu gave them a final word of advice: You will find . . . well, who knows what you will find, she corrected herself, smiling. (She did not want to tell them that their first image, after fully receiving the medicine, would in all likelihood be of two gigantic, entwined, perhaps copulating snakes.) But what happens to me is that just when I think nothing is happening and I'm shut outside of my experience with Grandmother, I will notice, sort of out of the corner of my eye, that there is a large brick wall or something like that. At first I will feel incapable of getting over,

around, or through it. Then I will remember that I can mentally
remove one of the bricks. I will do this. Suddenly I will find myself on the other side.

They were required to wear diapers! This had seemed un-
bearably funny to Kate. And amusing to realize she liked the
bulky feel of them between her legs. She was a baby again; she
realized how much she must have enjoyed being one. She seemed
to remember, feeling the diapers on her bottom, that when she
was a baby people were always kissing her. Um, she thought.
Happy.

This is to make sure you don't have an accident on your way
to the bathroom, said Anunu. She and her assistant, Enoba, a
white woman with dark hair and warm hazel eyes, took each of
them by the hand and walked with them from their lounges out
the door to the bathroom, just to make sure they would remember where it was.

Will we be forgetful as all that? asked Kate, worried.

We'll be right with you, said Enoba, whether you forget or
not. One of us will walk with you, just like now, and will stand
outside until you come out again.

When was the last time someone had stood outside the toilet waiting for her? Kate asked herself. Her mother, maybe,
when she was a child. Or perhaps a nurse, when she'd been in
the hospital having her children.

She liked it. Oh, she thought to herself, I am someone who
enjoys being pampered! Usually, raising her children, she'd received no such pampering, though always giving it to others.
She had forgotten her own need. And, she thought, I am wearing Pampers! She was having fun even before the journey.

Yolo Had Read

YOLO HAD READ ALL ABOUT HAWAII, THE HAWAII of surfing and volcanoes, before coming. He'd once even had a Hawaiian girlfriend. She was a gifted hula dancer and he'd met her at a party. She was with a very average sort of white guy and this white guy, looking ill at ease in so large and diversified a gathering, wanted her to dance.

I don't really want to, she said. She was smoking a cigarette and looking rather bored.

Ah, come on, he said.

I'm not dressed for it, she said. She was wearing a black turtleneck sweater, black woolen trousers, and a big brown leather bomber jacket. She shrugged out of the jacket and let it slide to the floor. Yolo had picked it up and flung it on a chair.

Ta da! the white guy said, pulling a bag from behind the sofa.

The woman looked at him and made a face.

They were all artists of one sort or another. Writers, painters, poets, musicians. All tipsy by now and easily entertained.

Yolo was hoping the sister would just say no to the idea

of performing. After all, it was a party thrown by the people whose home it was. She was a guest. Why couldn't she sit and chat and while away the time any way she felt like it?

The guy was persistent.

You're so great, he was whining. You ought to give these people a treat.

Yolo wondered if he should speak up. Then he found himself doing so.

They were standing close to the clam-dip tray, which was on a tall wooden table by the window. She wore her hair loose and billowing as Hawaiian women started to do again after the sixties. They'd been much influenced by Kathleen Cleaver of the Black Panthers and Angela Davis of the Black Liberation Movement, both women with exceedingly big hair. She seemed willowy and light beneath it.

You don't have to dance, he said, looking down at her. Ignoring the white guy, whose hand was on her arm. A hand that looked too white, really, to be there. But Yolo squelched that thought.

But by now the party had roused itself and become a single consciousness, as tipsy parties sometimes will, and that consciousness had heard the word *Hawaii* and that consciousness knew only one thing for sure about that place: There were beautiful brown women there, dancing.

It gives me great pleasure to introduce my date, Leilani. The white guy was clearly trying to introduce himself.

Yaay! yelled a very drunk man who had seated himself close to the vodka end of the tiny, well-stocked bar across the room.

Hardly seeming to move, the young woman tied a scarf around her head to resemble a haku lei and wriggled herself out of her sweater and trousers and into a pareo and bikini top. Her boyfriend had put on some Hawaiian music that sounded like warm syrup and she began to dance.

It looked like every hula Yolo had ever seen on TV. It also seemed really long. Her hands waved this way and then the other. Her hips swiveled. He thought that at one time, under the proper moon and palm trees, this dance had embodied both enchantment and desire. Now it seemed rote. Yolo wondered how she could keep the same smile plastered on her face the whole time.

There was no way to tell, from her smiling, complaisant mien, that she was angry.

He would never have guessed. Except that later, leaving the party, he heard an argument, a heated argument, going on as a couple approached their car down the street. He drew abreast of them just in time to see Leilani hit the white guy over the head with the bag that had held her dancing clothes, and to see him draw back and punch her. Yolo of course grabbed the guy, who immediately began to cry and to say how sorry he was.

Oh God, Leilani sneered, wiping a trickle of blood from her nose, a crier.

She was wearing highly polished black leather boots that glistened against the snow.

She unlocked the door of her car, a silver-colored SAAB, and prepared to slide in.

Wait, said the guy. I don't have a way home.

Tough, she said, spitting in the gutter near his feet. Take a fucking boat.

This seemed incredibly funny to Yolo, who began to laugh.

Soon they were all laughing.

I'm sorry, said the white guy, who introduced himself as Saul.

I'm not, said Leilani.

Yolo and Saul watched as she made a tight bun of her billowing hair, started her car, and almost ran over them driving away.

A Hawaiian in New England! said Saul, stamping his foot in the snow.

That would make a good title for a book, said Yolo.

He'd met her again several weeks later. On a street downtown. This time kicking a parking meter.

Is anything wrong? he'd asked.

She looked at him as if to say: Let me count the ways.

She had found a parking place, after driving around for half an hour, gratefully put her money in the slot, but now it would not go down. The big red "Expired" would signal the ever-circling meter maid who was notorious for giving large tickets.

I don't understand this civilization, said Leilani.

You know, Leilani, neither do I. Here, he said. I have a paper bag we can put over it.

It's so fucking cold, she said. Why do they have to charge people to park?

She took the paper bag and stuck it over the meter.

There, said Yolo. That means the meter maid will have to get out of her car and look under the bag. When she does that, she'll see your quarter.

My name isn't Leilani, she said. It's Alma.

What? he said.

Leilani is the name everybody thinks a Hawaiian woman should have. Especially if she dances hula.

I enjoyed your dancing, said Yolo gallantly.

Alma was again dressed all in black that matched her large

black eyes. Her long cashmere coat was buttoned up to her chin. On her head was a big black furry Russian-looking hat.

America was so Third World, Yolo thought, considering all the people from everywhere who now lived here. And then, catching himself, he thought: Hawaii is America. But he could not really believe this.

Over coffee and a Danish they properly introduced themselves.

Yolo? she asked

A Poewin Indian word, said Yolo. I gave it to myself. It means a place in the river where wild rushes grow, lots of them. I think of rushes as impulses, as energy. It suited me. My given name, by my parents, was Henry. Well, he said, taking a bite of his Danish, a Henry I am not. Besides, what does *Henry* mean?

Exactly, said Alma, who was named after a Hawaiian kahuna. I'm not really an Alma either, but it seems to take a while to find one's true name.

Alma means soul, said Yolo. That's not bad.

Still, said Alma.

Yolo looked at her intently, then closed his eyes. When he opened them he said: I get a fragrant wood for you, something precious, tall and straight, perhaps endangered.

Koa? she asked. Hmmm.

What is koa? he asked.

Just what you describe. Except, maybe not koa, but sandalwood? Some of our islands were covered with sandalwood trees. You could smell them far out to sea.

Were covered?

The forests were completely exploited. No trees at all are left. They went to Asia, Europe, America. They were made into incense, matchboxes, doodads.

Well, you wouldn't want to be called Sandal anyway, sounds too much like *shoe,* said Yolo.

She smiled, sadly.

Koa, though.

I like it, she said. It's gender-free, as well.

First of All, Abandon

FIRST OF ALL, ABANDON ANY NOTION THAT ANYTHING *you humans do will ultimately destroy me. That is because I am your mother. It is impossible to kill one's mother. You may shoot her a hundred times, but alas, she has already given birth to you. She is yours forever. What you are destroying is your own happiness. Your comfort, which I put so much playful effort into creating. Your peace of mind. Your joy.*

There is no potion, no poison you can create, that will do anything but rearrange the pattern I have made. And, let me add, you were created in such a way that you can do this. So destruction too is part of the overall design.

The biggest problem is thinking the fate of the world rests on you. It does, and it doesn't. The "saving" of the planet, as you humans think of it, can be done really easily. All that is required is that everyone becomes as one mind. The mind, actually, of clay, she said, and laughed. Television creates this global one mind to some extent, but the programming is so bad. Then there are the languages people have which have become a completely unnecessary division. There is no need to talk, really. It is something humans started a long time ago—I don't even remember why—and they've clung to it. Clinging to speech they've lost the ability to read one another, to feel one another, to know one another at a glance. Or with a sniff. It is entirely within human capability to do this.

When you witness the various peace talks that occur on a daily basis somewhere on earth and you see how far everyone is from peace, and how they get no nearer the longer they talk, well, this gives an indication of the problem.

If you see a human being, *really see them,* Kate thought, how could you kill them? Even more so if you smelled them. She thought about the peace talks she'd seen on television, the snippets of peace talks one saw on the news. Everybody arriving in limos, trying to look serious and important. But nobody wanted to smell or see anybody else. And by now the human smells of fear and suffering made humans angry. They thought they could wipe out fear and suffering if they destroyed their scent. Fear and suffering, that is always the smell of the enemy.

Don't you dare show me any fear, they seemed to say to one another. Act like nothing's happening that I should be frightened of! Act like you don't know I've bombed your house and you were terrified watching your grandmother bleed. Don't let me smell your grief. Smile! There's the camera. We're all men here, we've got to show we're on top of this thing.

This is what civilization really meant. What it came to, in the end. Abandonment of the animal fear of annihilation, the scent of suffering. Not wanting to see it in others, not wanting to face it in yourself. When these men left the peace talks they returned to the military bastion from which they directed their tanks. Blow up the memory of the fear in the eyes of the enemy, was the command. Blow it up before I feel it too deeply in myself. There was no way of not knowing, on some level, that the bombing left a hole in the bomber, made it necessary to evacuate himself.

There's your dad, come home from the war, run give him a kiss!

The child runs up, kisses the face of the man. Is puzzled. If she is young enough she smells and sees precisely. Where has he gone to, her dad?

How could it be otherwise?

Like Elizabeth Taylor

LIKE ELIZABETH TAYLOR, KATE HAD BEEN MAR-
ried many times. Some of these marriages had been very short.
Three had lasted about a year. The others, one in which she'd
borne children, were longer. When she met Yolo she was sworn
off marriage; that was one of the first things she said to him
when they discussed living together.

I can do the living-together thing very well, but being married is of no interest to me.

Cool, he'd said, kissing her.

It wasn't that she loved him less than any of those she'd
married; in fact, she felt she probably loved him more. It was
just that she couldn't bear to be wrong again. To wake up beside
one more person in the morning thinking: Who in the world is
this, and how on earth did he or she get in my bed? Her bed, a
massive thing draped in silk, was special to her. Analagous
really to a secret chamber of her heart. When this space was de-
filed, even by her own bad judgment, perhaps especially then,
she felt terrible, as if she'd been stabbed.

Walking through the rainforest on her way to the waterfall
where they bathed, she recalled one of her "marriages"; a short
one, that was particularly embarrassing to remember. She'd

fallen in love with a woman whom she'd mistaken for someone else; in fact, the woman had resembled an older relative who'd died, a cousin who had loved Kate and someone who, just by being, had made Kate laugh with delight. Lolly, the woman who resembled her cousin—twinkling eyes, lovely smile—turned out to be a hustler, someone who wheedled and cajoled until she got whatever it was she wanted. For the longest time Kate had been oblivious to this. Then fascinated and unbelieving. Sure her golden earrings and diamond necklace left to her by a great-aunt soon found their way onto Lolly's ears and around her neck. Soon enough they'd bought Lolly a new car while Kate made do with the jalopy. Still she couldn't quite believe none of her cousin's qualities of generosity and thoughtfulness existed in her. She realized much later, after they'd parted, that the experience with Lolly had been an attempt to deal with her considerable and inadequately expressed grief over her cousin's dying, far from her, and without leaving for her heart alone any special word.

They had married each other in a ceremony they designed at a friend's house on an island off the coast of the Carolinas. There beneath giant oak trees dripping moss they'd laughed to think they were expressing a freedom their forebears, who so desperately yearned for freedom from the lash, had not even imagined. And might well have been outraged by, though she doubted the more radical ones would have been anything but secretly amused. Kate was always willing to go far enough back in her ancestry to find the ones who resembled her; she knew they had to be there because look what they'd spawned. To honor the enslaved ancestors who had had to create their own wedding ceremonies, they'd jumped the broom, the only nuptials slave owners had permitted their African captives. Lolly was swathed in Kente cloth from head to toe. Kate had worn a white linen suit and a wide-brimmed white straw hat. And suede fawn-colored cowboy boots. Friends joked that they looked like Africa and Colonial America finally doing the right thing.

Their friends, Lolly's old girlfriends, her children, the odd relative, cheered when they kissed. There was a feeling of liberation that carried them for quite a number of months. Until Kate had begun to wonder whether Lolly ever intended to work. And whether she would ever get in the habit of rising before noon.

Kate was an early riser and worked steadily at her desk until noon, when she broke for lunch. Early in the marriage she'd hurry to the kitchen, make a light lunch, and carry it, on a tray, to the bedroom. Lolly always wanted freshly squeezed orange juice the moment she opened her eyes, and Kate always prepared it for her. They might cuddle for a bit, eat their lunch, looking out the sunny open bedroom door into the sun-splashed garden, and talk about what they'd like to do in the evening. A movie, the theater, a video, maybe dinner at someplace new? It was a way of life for which Kate had yearned. The children were grown up and away at school, her work supported her very nicely, her health was good, and none of her innate curiosity about and interest in life had ebbed. She also in no way subscribed to the rules and regulations of a society that suppressed almost all spontaneous signs of joy, and whose insistence on conformity, she had noticed, made life so lacking in vibrancy for all concerned. At the moment she realized any human being might die for almost any reason at any given instant, she also understood that, accepting this fact, she could be free.

She'd had no experience before with the problem Lolly confronted her with: contented laziness.

Lolly had been born, according to her, with a slight learning disability. Very slight, she'd say, grinning. Perhaps, she thought, dyslexia. But it had made her mother leery of ever letting her out of her sight. She was never to go anywhere alone. When she was growing up she heard her mother say to other people, people outside the family: Don't mind Lolly, she's simple. When she asked her mother what that meant, her mother had stroked her soft, silky hair, and said, It means I have to take better care of you, and look out more for you, than for the others. This had made Lolly feel special, though she sometimes wanted to go places by herself as her siblings did.

It was while shopping with her mother that she'd discovered her gift. In place of the "smartness" her mother identified in her other children, which meant they could go about on their own, she had been given an innate shrewdness. She could drive a swifter and harder bargain at the market than her mother. She could also calculate the cost of purchases faster.

She would stand in front of the fruit counter watching her mother pick over apples. When the merchant came up she'd say, in her open-faced, simpleton's way: Those apples are so mushy. I'm sure we could get harder ones at the market down the street. Or, she'd say, dragging out the words, and perhaps running her hands over all the apples in front of her, maybe they should be a little more cheap.

Soon it was as if her mother went to the market with her. And she shopped for the family until she left home with the teacher who had been hired to teach her remedial reading. A woman who was charmed by this small brown Venus, as she liked to call her, who seemed to ask for nothing directly but who could and did drop the most indelible hints.

At some point Kate realized the biggest hint being pitched was for her to sign over half of her house. Lolly, as if they were legally married, considered it community property. In every conversation, no matter what they talked about, even if it were about fleas on the dogs, who had to live somewhere, the subject of Lolly's fear of homelessness arose. Kate discovered a territoriality in herself she hadn't known was there. Half of her house, to someone who didn't work and didn't arise until noon? She didn't think so.

What was horrible was the feeling of having been taken. Of having been a chump. As she began to notice how Lolly operated in the world, she could see how mistaken she'd been ever to consider her helpless, which she had done, or, Goddess forbid, simpleminded. Lolly's mind worked like an abacus. *Click-click*. This is what I want and this is what I have to do to get it. Who has what I want? I'll go stand next to her.

Kate eased herself free, after a little more than a year. She watched as Lolly looked about, spotted another hardworking woman, sidled up to her with her stories of having grown up simpleminded and shrewd. And, oh yes, the thing I've most wanted in the world is my own house. You have one, I see.

At the Waterfall

AT THE WATERFALL SHE ENCOUNTERED LALIKA, the black woman from Mississippi who regularly broke down on her yagé journeys. Kate was now aware of everyone during the sessions because the medicine had ceased to work on her. She continued to sit with the others because Armando had asked her to; she was even able to help him, with a word, a fan, a musical instrument he wanted, from time to time. And she had become someone to whom the others turned, which surprised her.

Lalika had had her bath and was sitting by the side of the river, deep in thought. She gave a slight nod as Kate doffed her shorts and T-shirt and rushed under the falls. The water was refreshing. She tried not to think about what might be in it; after all, the fish they saw downstream would have dived over the falls, perhaps the crocodiles too. She made quick work of washing her hair, not bothering to add conditioner as she would have at home.

She spread a towel near Lalika, not so close that Lalika would feel the need to talk to her, and stretched out in the waning afternoon sun. Soon there would be too many bugs to be outside, but at the moment it was peaceful. There was a bluish tinge to the light in the clearing. She began to drift. Until she heard a sound.

Lalika, when she glanced at her, was weeping.

With a sigh, Kate turned her face away.

Do you think this stuff will help me? asked Lalika. Almost in a whisper. Kate had never heard a voice so forlorn.

You mean Grandmother? asked Kate.

Yeah, yagé. Lalika attempted a smile. *Grandmother.* Hmmm. I like that better, she said.

Kate knew a bit about Lalika's life because she was, in some quarters, infamous. Lalika was a murderer.

What is the thing you feel you need the most help with? asked Kate.

Lalika was quiet for so long Kate thought she hadn't been heard.

I need to feel like me again, said Lalika. And burst into tears. I miss myself so much, she said, her face as contorted as a child's.

At first Kate stayed still, reflective, on her towel. Then she sat up and hugged her knees. It was hard to let Lalika weep alone, but she let her continue for several minutes. Yes, she thought, just be alone with it. Feel the fucking pain to the core.

When the racking sobs began to subside Kate roused herself, went over to the river with her towel, and brought it back sopping wet. Wringing it out a bit, she draped it over Lalika's head which was hot from the sun and sweaty and ashen from crying.

Lalika grabbed the ends of the towel gratefully, tucking them under her chin.

Here we are in the middle of absolutely—who the hell knows where—

And, continued Kate, two of us have managed to be here.

Two of us are here. Lalika repeated this as if to herself. However, the thought seemed to arouse more sorrow and she began to cry fresh tears. In fact, she began to wail.

It seemed to Kate, as the wailing went on and on and began to reverberate through the jungle—and "jungle" was exactly what this rainforest was, impenetrable off the narrow trails they walked—that it had the curious effect of rousing the vegetation. That is to say, she felt as though the trees and bushes of the forest awoke. There was an attentiveness in the air. It was certainly not a human attentiveness, no one else was around. And yet it felt like Lalika's wailing had attracted a crowd.

Hmmm, she said to Lalika. Do you get the feeling we're not alone?

Lalika, whose head by now rested against Kate's shoulder, wiped her face with the rapidly drying towel, looked toward the river, listened intently to the humming sound of insects, and said, abruptly sitting up:

I feel so much better. Surprised.

Kate looked down at her. Lalika was in her mid-thirties, a common, ordinary black woman no one would look at twice on the street. In this setting she looked incredibly beautiful. Her skin resembled the earth, her hair looked like the trees. Her eyes had the deep light of the brown river.

You're really beautiful, said Kate.

Naw, said Lalika.

Yeah, said Kate.

They sat together, shoulders touching. The mosquitoes began to sound like airplanes. Lalika shared her insect repellant but the critters licked it off like icing before plunging their needles into them. They were so big and healthy killing one made Kate feel guilty.

They gathered their things and ran.

Thinking about yagé and how it no longer worked on her, Kate remembered a talk she'd heard by Ram Dass. He'd been a devotee of LSD and had thought it the most powerful tranformative substance in the world. He'd taken a lot of it to India the first time he went, thinking he'd try it on some of the gurus there. Kate appreciated his irreverence. He'd met "Baba," as he called the tiny Indian who became his guru, and within days Baba had asked about the "medicine" he'd brought. Ram Dass had never thought of it as that. Surprised that the old man even knew he had brought something, Ram Dass decided to give him a dose of LSD large enough to disorient several elephants. At last, he thought, I will be told what LSD really is. He hung around the tree under which Baba sat for hours, waiting to see what would be the effect. He waited and he waited.

Every once in a while Baba would look at him and smile, a twinkle in his eye.

Toward nightfall Ram Dass realized this was his answer. The powerful drug had no effect whatsoever on Baba; to him it was absolutely nothing.

Kate's first session with Grandmother had been seven hours long. She'd lifted the "brick," which was more like a scale on the side of a very large reptile, and gotten inside the world where Grandmother lived. It was as if Grandmother had been waiting thousands of years to take her onto her lap. The teaching had begun immediately.

But underneath the palapa in the jungle the same dose of yagé left her unmoved; she'd sat out the entire session wondering when it would begin for her. Other people were clearly on their trips. Armando and his apprentice shaman, Cosmi, were busy with their songs and rattles and fans and *agua florida*. She watched it all as if it were a play.

Lalika was holding herself rigidly, as if sitting in a runaway train, when Kate looked at her. The white woman next to her, short and slender with light brown braids wound around her head, was tossing about in her seat, eyes closed, moaning and crying. She had been incested from the time she could barely crawl. She had never been able to own this until she worked with Anunu. Now she owned it at every opportunity and had discussed it quite calmly in the dugout canoe that brought them to the camp. There was a deeper layer of suffering to be explored though, apparently, and she, already battered, was resisting it.

Kate was moved by the tenderness with which Armando and Cosmi held everyone. She thought about how, five hundred years before, the Spanish conquistadors might have encountered this same scene, almost exactly, as they hacked through the jungle looking for gold. Except all the participants would have been Indians, not just the shaman and his helpers. How surprised they'd be, she thought, if they could peek up at us from hell. She was certain that's where they were because that is what they had believed in. Coming upon the Indians prayerfully attempting to heal themselves, their healers as patient and loving as mothers, the smelly, unwashed, metal-plated, unwanted desperadoes of medieval Spain had set upon them with swords and dogs, killing them in the name of God. How many shamans, perhaps even more gifted than Armando, had the Spanish slain? How many had they taken captive, pressed into slavery? How many had died in the gold and silver mines?

And yet, here they were, tending the sick descendents of the people who'd almost destroyed them. Even their bodies, for hundreds of years, had not belonged to them. Armando and Cosmi carried the Indian spirit of their ancestors, but their bodies showed traces of the long Spanish domination, as did their last names.

A sick person has no history and no nationality, said Armando when they were discussing the past.

If you cannot feel that way there is no possibility of becoming a *curandero*.

Kate pondered this. She was still plagued by those ancestors of hers who'd lived and died miserably. They wanted her to rectify their wrongs, she felt. There were weeks when they seemed to visit her every night. For instance, there was the man with no teeth. A bloody mouth. He'd appeared to her in dreams but even more in wakeful visions.

Oh, no, she'd groaned, catching a glimpse of him the first time.

But there he was. Eventually she had to look.

And when you did look, asked Armando, gazing warmly into her eyes, what did you see?

Kate was quiet. Finally she said: I saw someone with a story to tell. Someone with a story to tell and someone who chose me, or was trying to choose me, to tell it.

The problem was, she continued, I did not want to relay any more sad messages from the other side.

L'otro lado? asked Armando.

You know, the Other World. Ancestor territory.

Oh, he said, and laughed. We do not get to decide something like that!

I know, she said, with a sigh.

He wanted me to know, especially, how good-looking he'd been. How *handsome*. He was vain, had been born that way. Even as a slave with no idea who his parents had been, he'd been pleased with how he looked. He'd sneak into the mistress's sewing room, where there was a mirror, and admire himself!

The inner spirit is never enslaved, said Armando.

I guess not, said Kate.

The way we are born, in that area, is just the way we are, he chuckled. Take it or leave it.

He was so beautiful, he thought. The mistress thought so too.

How do you say, *Oops,* said Armando.

Right, said Kate.

And unfortunately her husband, the master, was old and ugly and had those horrible English teeth. Rotted right down to the crooked roots. The English always had bad teeth during those centuries. They had such bad food and poor dental hygiene. The whole of Europe was constipated.

Really? said Armando, immediately thinking of a cure, Kate was sure.

And our man, not so long out of Africa where his people were accustomed to a really good diet, had perfect teeth. Though a slave he had perfect teeth. And these perfect teeth were praised by the mistress, who, not being brave enough to try to fuck him (excuse me), could and did rave about his big, strong white teeth.

Needless to say, Old Master was not amused. Being both almost toothless and entirely impotent.

Kate felt she could not go on. Though Armando was listening to her with a tenderness that encouraged each word. They were sitting on the ground near the palapa. He'd spread a large straw mat for them and while they waited for her to continue he leaned back on his elbow. She noticed some gray hairs on the side of his head and in his small mustache. His hair had grown since they arrived and was almost to his shoulders. Very strong, thick, glistening hair that had always flourished in this latitude, this humidity, this air.

He—the Master—had them pulled out, Kate said flatly. His beautiful white teeth. One by one, with the pliers they used for horses, without anesthesia. As she said this, she felt physically sick, her whole body went into shock, like a plant being pulled up by the roots.

Armando nodded. Take my hand, he said.

Kate placed her hand in his.

Armando began to sing.

He sang low and solemn, holding Kate's hand, until everyone in the camp had come out of their huts or their spots by the river, and gathered silently around them. Everyone listened to the amazing thing Armando's singing was. Most of them knew not one word of the language he was singing in. Perhaps Kechua or Mayan. It didn't matter. They felt the soul of it. They intuitively felt it was that rare, audacious yet respectful song that dared to ask mercy of the ancestors. Reminding them that those of us still living already have many burdens to bear. That a time comes when we have done all we can do. We have done enough. That it is perhaps not entirely right to continue to petition the loving souls among us, those who will try to do everything we are asked. There is as well the temperament of the person to be considered, the song seemed to say. Is it right to break the hearts of those who would honor us, by requiring them to sleep, without rest, with our own bad dreams?

Kate was weeping and, astonishing to her, the tears seemed to be coursing down her arm, hot, like blood, and into Armando's hand. When she looked, she saw it was true. Her left shoulder, her arm, her hand, were all dripping water as if Armando's song had pierced the heavy, water-logged region of her heart. Her chest, which had been stretched high with grief and sadness, began to fall. She began to breathe. Deeply. Feeling an inner space. A clarity.

Cosmi had arrived with a rattle and a flute. As Armando continued to sing, he offered a sweet accompaniment, first with the rattle, then with the flute.

Kate remembered the poet Jane Stembridge, of the Movement for Black Freedom in Mississippi so many years ago. A white woman who was pushed out of the struggle in the South because some black people were so devastated by the past they could not forgive it. When they looked at Jane they never even saw her. They saw mistresses who'd caused them pain. But Jane in her book *I Play Flute* had asked a crucial question: Where is the sound of the flute, she had written, that ushers freedom in?

Kate had respected Jane for not letting herself be stuck in someone else's image of her, but recognized instead that her very Being, white and female and descended from slave owners though it was, might be a note of freedom. And the Women's Movement, emerging later, which uncovered and named the camouflaged enslavement at the root of white women's lives, had proved her right. One's struggle against oppression is meaningless, she had known, unless it is connected to the oppression of others.

Kate was exhausted by the time Armando's song was completed. She wanted only to sleep. Armando turned to Cosmi and asked him to bring her a special medicine. He explained to Kate, as Cosmi approached with a pitcher full of an earth-colored liquid, that this medicine, Bobinsana, would help her have lucid dreams. And in her lucid dream tonight, she would be able to talk in the right way to her ancestor.

You will not have fear, he said. You will not have guilt. You will be able to state clearly your love of him but also your need to be free.

The hard work will be, he added gravely, letting go of your need not to be free. Because you see, even though today everybody talks about ancestors in a somewhat lofty way—ancestor this, ancestor that—they are actually very much like one's siblings. He laughed. Some of them need to be negotiated.

When the Spaniards came they made a game of slicing our people in two. We'd never seen a sword, you know. And they must have thought killing us in this way was entertaining. They fed our babies to their dogs. What they did to women is perhaps better unsaid. We are left with the record and the consequences of this behavior in our own bodies and psyches, and we must work with it. Not because it is Spanish behavior, no. Because it is human behavior. And we too are humans.

It will never work to think we are exempt from madness. I think you will be surprised to learn what it is this ancestor wants to tell you. He merely hooked you with that stuff about vanity. And why? Because he knows you are vain. Vanity interests you. But there is more to the story, I can assure you.

Kate was so sleepy by now that she staggered. Lalika stepped forward and placed an arm around her waist. The woman who always sat next to Lalika in circle, who was actually called Missy, came up to support her on the other side. In this odd threesome they tottered along the path, through the forest and toward Kate's tiny hut.

Mistress Kate, he said, *you can have no idea how long it takes to die. Even if it is all over in an instant. Time is relative, and you really understand it when you're dying.*

In the dream they were in the countryside, a countryside that showed no signs of modernity. Kate was standing on a road, a rough dirt road, quite narrow, and he was sitting beside it, not on the ground, but suspended in the air. His bloody gums, which had always seemed to lunge toward her out of his mouth, were now barely visible, though flashes of a ragged redness revealed nothing had changed. He didn't seem to be showing her his wound. But was intent, instead, on telling her something he knew.

Why am I Mistress Kate? she asked primly.

He shrugged. *You are not a slave. You are wearing shoes.*

Oh, she said, looking down at herself. It was true; on her feet were Birkenstock sandals. And she was wearing a frilly white dress.

Here's a parasol, he said, handing her an acorn.

She laughed because there was a parasol on its top. Every acorn was shaped that way; to protect itself from the rain. Rain rot.

My death took several lifetimes, he said. *During which I felt every moment of my life in which I could have been better.* Horrible. *And yet, I was shot through the heart. Killed instantly, they said. They hated I'd been killed instantly, they'd hoped to have some fun with me.*

By "they" do you mean . . . ?

Night riders, he said.

Even though she knew she was dreaming, and could see her dreaming body lying under the mosquito net on her narrow bed, Kate felt herself draw back.

It is not what you think, he said. He paused. *Rather, it is exactly what you think. Yes, there were centuries of terrorism, and this was a common incident. The nigger running, the white fiends chasing. The sound of the dogs. They were curiously inept at creating entertainment for themselves that didn't center around us. I imagine this has not changed.*

Aw, naw, you shot 'im through the heart. One of them said this, as they stood looking down at me. And you know what, so disappointed was he to be robbed of the good time he'd looked forward to, of torturing me, that he turned on the man who shot me and hit him. Right there, as I was dying, they began to fight.

This is what I want you to remember, he said. *Not how painful having my teeth pulled out must have been.*

Kate shook her head.

I don't understand, she said.

We are very old, our people. Not many could have suffered as we have and survived. We have had many lifetimes as human beings to learn of the many, many ways we do not wish to be.

But we are human, she said, *and therefore we already are every way there is.*

That's true, he said, *but there is still a bit of room for choice. Which is why it is worthwhile to remain in contact with your ancestors.*

They were now walking on the same road, side by side. A pale, full moon was setting.

Did you realize ancestors have jobs? he asked.

I bet the slaves who died didn't want to hear that! she said, and laughed.

He smiled, and a bit of blood dropped in the red dirt.

Do you think when a tree dies all its work is finished? Of course not. It then has the work of decomposing, of becoming soil in which other trees grow. It is very careful to do this, left to itself, and not hauled off to a lumberyard. If it is hauled off to a lumberyard and if nothing is left to decompose and nurture the young trees coming up . . . Disaster!

She thought of clear-cutting. Clear-cuts she had seen along the Klamath River in northern California. The landscape that had been so lush and powerful was left bare and desolate; the young trees coming up had no shade to protect them from the blistering sun that baked the earth to ash. They were as brittle as matchsticks and unable to grow tall. They would never know the grandeur of the parents and grandparents who preceded them. How would they ever guess what their true nature was?

Our job is to remind you of ways you do not want to be, he said. *Sometimes I think this message is the hardest to get across because it flies in the face of our need to have revenge. There is also the question of loyalty to the dead. We feel we need to avenge, to make right. To heal by settling a score. Healing cannot be done by settling a score.*

As he said this, he laughed, as if the very thought were absurd. Blood flew all over the place, some of it flecking her white dress. But in just that moment her dress changed into a buffalo skin and the flecks of blood didn't show. Hmmm . . . she thought. Looking down, for just a moment, there was a hoof.

What's your name, by the way? she asked.

Remus, he said.

Remus? Like Uncle Remus? You're kidding.

No, he said. *I know that name is considered a joke by some people. It was a common name for slaves. The masters liked it because it made us seem ridiculous.*

The original Remus was suckled by wolves, she said, *and with his brother Romulus, he founded the city of Rome.*

Really, he said. *I've never been to Rome.*

Where have you been? she asked.

Only here, he said. *Only with you.*

They were now passing an enormous field of corn. Remus was barefoot and wearing ragged gray cotton trousers. Kate walked behind him looking at his footprints. Each time he lifted his foot one print would fill with water and the other with blood.

In the one that filled with water she saw her own face.

They sat abruptly at the side of road near the cornfield. Kate found an ear of corn in her hand. She began to strip its husk.

I used to have to plant, harvest, shuck, and shell a field of corn this size every year, said Remus. *After shucking so much corn it took the rest of winter for the palms of my hands to heal, to grow new skin. Consequently, I hate corn.*

No, you don't, said Kate. *You hate having been forced to deal with it. Corn is innocent. It had nothing to do with enslaving you.*

Remus looked down at her. *Who's the ancestor here?* he joked.

We living have jobs too, she said, beginning to pull the silver hairs from the gleaming pearl-colored ear of corn in her hands. It did not surprise her that as she did this, the ear of corn became hard as a rock. Or rather, hard as dried corn. She knew immediately what she was to do.

She took the hand of Remus, a hand as dry and scratchy as the bark of a tree.

Here, she said, handing him the ear of corn. *Eat this.*

Remus made a face.

Go ahead, she insisted. *Eat it.*

He bared his gums.

Eat it, Remus.

I have nothing to eat it with, he said, *even if I wanted to.*

Oh ye of little faith, she said. *Just see what you can do with it, to please me.*

It's so hard, he said, taking the ear of corn.

Yes, it is, she said.

She watched as Remus, only to please her, put the hard, dry ear of corn into his mouth. Blood smearing it as he did so, he clamped down, as if taking a bite. The kernels of corn immediately flew off the cob and attached themselves to his gums.

Remus, said Kate, beginning to chuckle at the astonished look on his face, *you now have a full set of teeth.*

He ran this way and that, looking for a mirror.

Here, she called after him. *Here is the mirror. Look in my eyes.*

When Remus looked into her eyes and saw himself, his beaming new smile, his happiness seemed to make him weak. He stumbled and began falling forward, into her. She felt the heaviness of him, his hard head, his broad shoulders, even his scratchy hands, passing into her chest. They seemed to be falling into a place just coming into view, far below them. She strained to see where they would fall, fearful they would be hurt. Though he was now inside her, she no longer felt his weight. And suddenly she saw clearly where they would land; it was her bed. Where she saw herself lying peacefully, sound asleep.

The Longer Yolo Kicked Back

THE LONGER YOLO KICKED BACK IN HIS LOUNGER
on the beach, just in front of the pale beige resort hotel, the
more he began to feel himself stuck on the surface of a façade.
What was behind this tranquil site in which he had been so disturbed? he wondered. Each morning he rose, donned his trim
green bathing trunks, took up his book—delighted to find himself enjoying a tale about goddesses and the tenacity of an
ancient Goddess religion—and plopped himself, with a jug of
lemonade at his elbow, in the shade of his beach umbrella. He
could not forget the face of the young man with whose body
he'd sat, however. He found his mind drifting as he gazed
toward da locals' section of the beach. He realized he knew almost nothing about Hawaii, beyond the reading he'd done before he came, whose sole intention had been to make of him a
contented tourist; there was no way of guessing the beginning of
the life whose ending he had seen. Thinking about it eventually
forced him from his seat by the sleep-inducing sea, and into the
bright red car he'd rented shortly after he arrived.

His car was red because he loved red. He was a Taurus, and
every other Taurus he knew also loved red and owned a red car.
In fact, he was often comforted while driving to see so many of

his kindred charging down the road. Like bulls they liked to take off with a kick of the back wheels and to storm the highway as if the curtain of landscape glimpsed through the windshield were the cape of the matador.

Where was he going, though? He had no idea. Once away from the hotel the place didn't even look like Hawaii. There were a lot of hardened lava flows that made the air hot and stifling, and after he'd passed those he came to yellowing grassy fields that looked like they'd been burned. A few minutes later he entered a forest of iron trees that resembled scraggly pines. Seconds later he was passing a cattle ranch. Patches of green grass looked like verdant postage stamps and the minuscule watering holes glinted in the sun. Next the sun disappeared and he found himself on top of a hill and in a mist so dense it almost turned into rain.

As his car dipped down into a small, breezy village, Yolo found himself bringing up the rear of a long line of slowly moving vehicles. The ones farthest from him were turning off the road. When he drew abreast of the turn he found himself at a small green church that looked like a child's drawing of one. Some of the cars turning to park in the church parking lot had their lights on. He realized he had come upon a funeral procession.

Driving very slowly he gazed at the gathering of people getting out of their cars. He recognized Jerry and the brother of the young man who had died. Out of surprise and respect, he slowed the car even more and pulled over to the side of the road.

What Is Missing from the World

WHAT IS MISSING FROM THE WORLD IS THE GRAND-
mother, Anunu had said. Oh, there are plenty of grandmothers,
little *g*, but Grandmother, big *G*, is impossible, some women
feel, to find. That is the absence that makes us afraid, she added.

It's quite an absence, said Kate. And will we find Her in
time?

Looking out the window behind Anunu's desk she watched
a blue jay pecking at a banana slug. The slug was the largest
she'd ever seen and the blue jay was making a joyful meal of it.
Soon another jay came and they began to fight. Another arrived,
and another. Soon there was a general melee. She was amazed to
see the much-pecked banana slug slowly gathering itself amid
the confusion and making its getaway. She laughed.

Anunu gazed at her.

Life, said Kate. It doesn't pay to give up on it too soon.

Someone had told Kate that Anunu was sixty-five years old.
She looked thirty-five. Her skin was smooth and vibrant, her
eyes clear and twinkling. Her body strong and lithe. How could
this be? Kate scrutinized Anunu carefully.

There is a time in every woman's life when she realizes the
absence of Grandmother, Anunu was saying.

Every woman? asked Kate.

Yes, said Anunu. Although sometimes, most times, the woman will think of it as something else. Some women will suddenly begin to dream of horses. Some will find big black bulls all over their dreams. Naturally this seems quite shocking to them, she said, laughing, though the bull is an early symbol of the Grandmother's ability to provide sustenance. Preceding the bull would have been the cow. Some women will find themselves entering a dance and not knowing how to do it because there is no teacher and the music, though hauntingly familiar, is impossible to follow. Some people will dream of water, vast expanses of water; they will not be able to swim because they don't know how and there will be no boat. Some people will begin to dream of rivers, but they will be dry.

I began to dream of dry rivers, said Kate. I took myself down the Colorado in a boat.

And did you find Her? asked Anunu.

Kate thought for a moment. That journey seemed to be more about emptying myself of the past, she said. A lot of my past lives came up, literally, in vomiting, there in the depths of the canyon, revealed for what they were. Dress rehearsals, in a sense, for some later phase of life. I felt, at the end of the trip, as we walked away from the river, that everything I'd carried up to that point that wasn't necessary to my life had been shaken loose. I was freed into this part of my life which, amazingly, has people like you in it.

Why is that amazing? asked Anunu.

Once when we were journeying, maybe eating peyote or mushrooms, said Kate, I saw you as I feel you've always been, through countless ages.

Really? said Anunu.

Yes, said Kate. It was during the period when I was just be-

ginning to understand I no longer needed to take any kind of
medicine. I lay there, wide awake, for the most part, unengaged
by whatever that particular medicine was. But there was a moment when I glanced over at you and Enoba and you were wearing your headdress of feathers.

A headdress of feathers?

Yes. Do you even own one? asked Kate.

Anunu laughed. No, but I'll certainly get one now.

They were green and red and purple feathers, and you had
worn them much longer than you've worn Western clothing. It's
amazing to me that time is so conflatable, said Kate. No doubt
we've done this sort of thing together before.

It no longer seemed strange to her that she was outside the
medicine loop. In the mornings Kate woke early to record her
dreams, drink her morning cup of Bobinsana, and walk down
to the river to bathe. She had decided not to worry about piranhas or crocodiles but to concentrate instead on her inner
peacefulness. She began to have the feeling that it was this inner
peace that attracted peace around her. If she approached the
river in this frame of mind, she felt sure no creature would
bother her.

Under the palapa she was now much needed. It wasn't that
she was asked to do anything specific; she was mostly required
to be present.

Armando had asked her about the sadness of Lalika and
been surprised and saddened to learn she had killed a man.

A bad man, said Kate.

Armando looked skeptical.

He had raped her and was trying to rape her friend.

Oh, he said.

In the circle Kate watched as Lalika, under the influence of the medicine, sat with tears streaming down her face.

After the killing she and her friend had tried to escape but they'd been captured and thrown into small, windowless country jail cells. They were beaten by the patrolmen who'd caught them and once inside the jail were raped repeatedly, over several months, by jailers and inmates alike. There had been a surveillance camera in their cells and they had been watched night and day. The beatings and brutal rapes had been preserved on video and marketed by two of the guards. There had not been one moment of privacy until word had finally gotten out about their condition and legal assistance from out of state had come to their aid.

When Lalika had tried to tell her the story Kate had asked, during a pause, whether she'd had therapy.

Lalika had laughed, the only time she did so.

Now she watched as Lalika writhed on the floor across from her. She seemed to be trying to escape from her own body.

Kate rose and knelt beside her. Out of Armando's way, as he sang over her, and out of Cosmi's way, as he blew on a burning twig that released billows of pungent smoke. The smoke covered them like a shroud and Kate realized they were indeed at the beginning of something dying. Looking at Armando to ask permission, which he with a nod gave, Kate took Lalika's hand. It was dry and cold, as if already dead. Lalika's eyes had rolled back in her head.

Armando was singing a song about forgiveness.

Who is it that most needs forgiving?
Who is it that feels so much pain?
Who is it that would really like to fly

Far far away?
Who is it that can return
Free and gentle
Like the rain?
It is the Self, my love,
My adored one,
It is the Self
That even now
Is running for its Life
Running to its life
Into the arms
Of death.
But we are here
The little sweet friends
Of the Self
And we are holding
On to nothing
But the Self
And we are saying
Beloved
Come back.

He sang this song over and over. Kate, whose time in her hut after dinner every night was spent, with Cosmi's help, translating Armando's songs from Kechua or Mayan into Spanish and then into English, began to weep herself, from the beauty of Armando's voice. When she had first heard his voice on a recording played for her by Anunu, she'd been unable to tell whether he was male or female. She'd thought him very old. He was young though, only in his forties. How was it possible he felt confident, in healing others, to attempt so much?

Was it because the world was in such bad shape, the young

must activate the ancient within themselves and the older must activate youth? On a spiritual level was there any difference?

I could not avoid killing him, Lalika had said. He was so huge. When I hit him with my fist he laughed. When I kicked him in the balls he said he felt excited. He wanted to fully experience himself, he said, and that was only possible with a nigger. Kate, Lalika had said, looking sadly into her eyes, what does that mean?

He thought he needed a perpetual victim, said Kate, in order to feel like a winner. He thought he was incapable of being himself on equal terms with a person of color. He thought he would be lost. What he had is by definition an inferiority complex.

They'd sat on a mat outside Lalika's hut. Lalika had brought with her to the Amazon a tiny piece of crocheting, creamy white and dainty. As she talked, she worked steadily, her needle smooth and silent. If I survive this journey, she told Kate, I will shave my head. Then, until I'm used to being bald, I will wear this little crocheted cap. It has many tears woven in, Lalika said thoughtfully, but if I live, the sun will dry them.

Kate had smiled, though tears came to her eyes.

It was so like women to create their own rituals, she thought, their own little markers of transition, their own ephemeral celebrations. Catching a tear as it slid down her own cheek Kate leaned forward and pressed it into Lalika's design.

There will be the tears of two of us, then, she said.

Lalika burst into tears.

Why does the thought that two of us will always be present make you cry? she asked.

Because it reminds me of Saartjie, said Lalika.

The Mourners Outside the Church

THE MOURNERS OUTSIDE THE CHURCH SEEMED TO be waiting for something. Yolo thought perhaps they waited for the priest, whose pickup truck was parked behind him. Yolo, regretting the brazen red of his car, watched as the priest, a middle-aged white man with salt-and-pepper hair, climbed down from his truck, carefully holding his skirt to avoid tripping over it. He watched as he walked heavily into the churchyard, greeting those assembled and stopping briefly to chat with several of them. Yolo watched as something was explained to him and he, like everyone, turned to look down the road.

As they all looked, Yolo heard a distant buzzing. Soon he saw someone approaching on a motorcycle. Though it was a warm, breezy day, this person was wearing a brown leather bomber jacket, black trousers, and black leather boots. Her billowing hair was pressed back from her face by the wind. Yolo rubbed his eyes.

He watched as his old girlfriend Alma, considerably heavier than when he'd last seen her twenty years before, alighted from the motorcycle, unzipped her jacket, reached inside, and brought forth a small silver urn. Holding the urn in front of her, as if it were a candle, she led the procession into the church.

Yolo could remain no longer on the postcard that had been his vacation. Wishing he'd worn something more suitable than shorts and a lighthearted shirt, he stumbled from his car, still astonished to see Alma in this setting, and made his way into the tiny church.

Inside, he sat at the very back. Alma was being greeted very warmly by everyone she passed. Many people embraced her. She seemed much older, ravaged by the years since he'd last seen her. There was a stoniness that surprised him. She moved jerkily, carefully raising a foot, carefully putting it down. Yolo watched as she placed the urn on the altar. He wondered if the young man who'd died was her son.

It was an overdose, of course, she told him later as they sat on her lanai sipping beers. She lived in a rambling house that had a wide corridor down the center of it, a breezeway, that opened out toward the ocean. And indeed, the breeze that traversed the island constantly moved through it. It was a breeze that lifted Alma's jet-black hair, in which not a thread of gray was seen, and covered them with the scent of flowers and fallen, overripe, mangoes.

I'm still astonished that I should be sitting here with you, said Yolo. And that I was one of the last people to sit with your son. He was very good-looking, he added.

Alma drew in a breath and followed it with a drag on her cigarette. She'd taken off the jacket and slacks and was now wearing a pareo and tank top. Her dark eyes were swollen from crying. Her hand shook as she removed the cigarette from her lips. Just behind her on the wall was a large faded poster of James Dean. He was looking, as usual, troubled and ill at ease.

Alma followed Yolo's gaze.

My father worshiped James Dean, she said. He wanted to be just like him.

What, said Yolo, without thinking: crazy and fucked up? Or gay?

The old Alma would have laughed.

Now she took a swig of her beer, opening another bottle as she drained the one she had.

He died like him, she said.

Yeah? said Yolo.

Ran his motorcycle over a cliff. Into the sea.

Really?

It's his jacket I wear. The motorcycle I bought myself.

Do you like it very much?

Alma shrugged. It's my ceremonial gear, she said. Like a tuxedo, where you come from. I wear it for all special occasions where it is important that my father's influence is acknowledged. My mother died when I was three. She was Hawaiian.

Your father wasn't? said Yolo in surprise.

German and Portuguese, she said. Other things too no doubt; you know how mixed-up Hawaiians are. But those two they claimed and tried to implement.

They were sitting on a wicker sofa on the lanai. Yolo lit another cigarette and threw the one he had been smoking into the ashtray, shaped like a mongoose, on the table in front of them. The mongoose had been brought to the islands to eat some pest or other, he seemed to recall from one of his tourist brochures, but the pest slept during the day and the mongoose at night. Or vice versa. So they'd become friends and waved briefly at one another in the late afternoon. Now the island was overrun with them and he'd heard they ate up people's chickens.

They were like . . . overseers, really, said Alma. A separate class. They are the ones that got land without having to buy it, for instance, after Hawaiians like my mother's people had their communal lands taken away from them and were placed on plantations to work. Along comes my dad, who's given everything a young white boy could want. Clothes, money, cars, motorcycles. Except all he wants is to be James Dean. And after only one movie.

Yolo laughed.

That's how slim the pickings were around here for a role model for someone like him. Hot-tempered, crazy, a European though born in the tropics. Whenever they traveled to the mainland dozens of people were sure to tell him how lucky he was. Just to be Hawaiian. Just to live in Hawaii. Paradise. *Rebel Without a Cause?* You bet.

With a sigh of exasperation, she rose to answer the phone, which had been ringing since they arrived. When she returned she was carrying two fresh beers and a plate of sashimi. On the floor near her feet there were already three empty bottles. His own bottle, though warm by now, was still half full. He took the cold bottle of Corona she offered and rubbed it across his forehead.

They wanted to send him "back East," as they called it, to college. Never mind that he hated school and all its works. They figured that out there in the "back East" he'd find a woman like himself. And I'm sure there were many back there like him too.

Yolo smiled at the face Alma made.

Parents, he said.

Well, he wasn't having it. First thing they knew he'd spotted a pure Hawaiian beauty over among the pineapples on Dole's plantation and the second thing they knew he wanted to marry her. *Olé!* All hell broke loose. Alma snickered. But it was too late because I was already lying in wait, planning on being born.

What was the overdose of, do you think? asked Yolo, relinquishing his half-full bottle of beer and taking a sip of the fresh, cold one.

Ice, maybe, she said. Crystal methamphetamine. It's the latest drug to swamp the island. So many of the young people are addicted to it. It fries the brain. Really, almost exactly the way an egg is fried. Marshall, my boy, hated being hooked. She took a fresh pack of Marlboros from a cabinet near the small wooden table in front of them. He started using on a dare, she said, tearing open a pack and lighting a fresh cigarette.

They were quiet, looking out at the ocean.

Where does it come from? Yolo asked. This is an island.

She looked at him coolly. Like nearly everything else, she said, it comes by boat.

Naturally

NATURALLY, SAID LALIKA, THERE CAME A TIME DUR-
ing our ordeal when we knew our only hope was to pray. I
asked Saartjie, Do you believe in God? She said no. We discussed this problem for a little while. We didn't have much time
because the guards let us out of our cells and into the yard for
only fifteen minutes. It was the only time during the day that we
saw each other. By then I loved the sight of her more than my
life. She was a large, bosomy woman with a big butt and a slow
smile. Not that either of us smiled much in jail. We'd met in the
field picking peaches with other migrant workers, though most
of the others were from Mexico.

We have to have somebody to pray to, she said. Jesus, I suggested. He suffered.

Maybe, she said, but with a tone that Jesus didn't quite get
it for her. He had a father, she said, looking away from me.

It wasn't long after that that one of the other prisoners lent
us a *Jet* magazine. You know how *Jet* can be counted on to tell
you the unglossed good and bad of the black race. And in this
issue there was the story of Saartjie Bartmann.

Really? said Kate. Wondering what *Jet* had had to say.

Just the bare bones, said Lalika. How she'd been taken from

South Africa by someone who put her in an exhibition because of her physical "deformities." Which were the norm in the tribe she was from. How she'd been dubbed the "Hottentot Venus" and forced to show herself to incredulous Europeans all over Europe. How when she died in childbirth she and the child were still dragged, embalmed and in an open coffin, around Europe. How parts of her body were cut off, pickled, and kept in a jar, ending up in a Paris museum.

Amazing, said Kate.

Typical, we thought.

And to have only that to read while you were being abused, said Kate.

Exactly, said Lalika. They were sitting on a log that had washed up when the river overran its path. Though it never rained in October, according to Armando, rain seemed imminent. The sky was filled with dark gray, water-saturated clouds. There was no wind. The heat was stifling.

A week or so after we read about Saartjie Bartmann each of us began to dream of her. It happened first to Gloria; that was her name before. She ran up to me and said: Guess who came to see me last night, right in the middle of . . . She didn't finish the sentence. I knew what she meant. I wasn't even asleep, she said. And there she was, the woman from *Jet* magazine.

I had almost forgotten. What woman from *Jet*? I asked her.

Saartjie, she said. The woman they cut up. She made a face. Our captors often threatened us with knives.

Oh, I said.

She just appeared, right in the middle of the room. One of them was on me, the other one trying to film it. She was so real I couldn't believe they didn't see her. We locked eyes, she said.

You did what! Girl, you're tripping, I said.

It happened, she said, all excited. You should have been there!

And then what? I said.

Gloria looked toward the sky with a dreamy kind of look and said, She was holding a jar with something in it.

Oh-oh, I said, mocking her.

And she had such a look of love on her face. Oh, it went right through me. She laughed, bitter and short. They thought I was responding to them.

I made a gagging gesture with my finger down my throat.

Really, she said.

We were running out of time. What was in the jar? I asked.

I don't know, she said. I was so busy looking at her face which was just like the face of a mother. A mother looking at her child. Not just her child, but her favorite, best, child.

And then, she raised the jar level with her heart, said Gloria, and it disappeared into her heart.

Maybe it was because she told me about it, said Lalika, gazing at the sky and then toward the river, which ran casually, unhurried, waiting for the rain, but the same night, Saartjie came to me. By then they were charging each other to use us.

She came to me as two of them were fighting over whose turn it was. She was dressed in clothing strange to me. A yellow grass skirt, a beautiful rose-colored shawl, and a big round red hat. And she was holding this glass jar in her hands, as if holding it out to me. Just for me to see it, nothing more. And she held me with that look. I never had a mother so I don't know if this is what my mother would have looked like if she'd managed to get inside that jail to try to comfort me. But the look on Saartjie's face was pure love. It was so extraordinary I forgot all about my body lying there exposed on the cot, and just as Gloria had done, I locked eyes with her. She was a big woman; big tits, big ass, big everything, I guess. I could see why the puny Europeans who first saw her naked body must have felt fear. If she could have so much—you know, tits, ass, pussy—why did they have so little?

Kate chuckled.

Aw, she's out, one of the guards said. For I had fallen into a kind of faint. And they threw cold water on me.

An odd rain was beginning to fall. Huge drops but several feet apart. Kate had never experienced anything like it. One drop fell on her head, steadily, as if all the drops for that spot were connected, and beyond her feet, like water dripping from a hose, another elongated drop. She and Lalika pondered the pattern of the rain without comment.

Maybe we should move, Lalika finally said.

I know, said Kate. Only, I don't want to.

I don't either, said Lalika. Settling her body more comfortably on the log and situating her head under a stream of the large drops. Soon her face and shoulders glistened with the rain. A burst of thunder so loud it almost dislodged them from their seat seemed to roll out of the forest. A restless wind began to eddy about their legs. A lightning that split the sky lit up everything around them.

Shall we sit? asked Kate.

Yeah, said Lalika. And she continued her story.

From that time on, we disappeared from our captors. We did not fight them. We did not curse them. We did not even try to ignore them. All of which we had done before. They did whatever they did to our bodies but we had flown. Into that voluminous grass skirt.

Kate smiled.

Into that big red round hat.

Kate laughed.

Into that rose-colored cape that seemed to be made of thorns.

Oops, said Kate.

Lalika said, Yes. It was the mammy cape. Surely made of thorns. But I don't mind the connection with Jesus. And besides, when I touched it, and I did touch it, the thorns did not prick me. They were as soft as flower petals. The cape itself as sheltering as a house.

And Gloria and I knew we had found our savior. Someone to pray to. Someone who answered prayer.

Lalika laughed, really laughed, without regret or bitterness, for the first time.

One day she called me Saartjie. And from that day never called me anything else. And then I started calling her Saartjie. And that is what we called each other, as if we were two expressions of that one loving and constant being, all of us with one name. We began to pray to Her. To Saartjie who, through *Jet* magazine, had come to us. We designated her a saint.

By now the log they sat on was slippery and glistening with rain. The huge single drops had been joined by a million others and pelted them like hail. Thunder continued to roll, lightning fiercely streaked the sky. Lalika gave herself to the pelting, squeezing her eyes tight and raising her face and chest to receive it. What a storm we're in, she said at last, turning her face to Kate.

And two of us are in it, said Kate. She could not tell, because of the rain on Lalika's face, if this comment provoked tears. She did not think so.

I Am Peace

I AM PEACE, SAID GRANDMOTHER. AND NOTHING HAS to die for me to exist. Not tobacco, not grapes or sugarcane. Not human beings. And not me! she added, laughing. When you circle, paint your faces with yagé to remember this.

James Dean Was the Only

JAMES DEAN WAS THE ONLY AMERICAN MAN MOST
Hawaiian men could identify with. Maybe because he was
smallish. In certain light, tan-ish. He walked like a Hawaiian,
not that used to wearing shoes. John Wayne or Fred Astaire
definitely wouldn't have come to mind, except for my grandfather and his cronies. That's my guess, said Alma. Here we
were in the middle of the Pacific, halfway between the United
States and Japan. They were fighting over us. Not because they
wanted us. They wanted the land. Not for its own sake. For
what they called "strategic purposes." The Americans made it
illegal for us to speak our own language. They sabotaged, ar-
rested, and dislodged our queen.

Like most tourists Yolo had a vague memory of a Hawaiian
queen but couldn't recall a thing about her. Certainly not her
name.

Lili'uokalani, said Alma. If his ignorance distressed her she
did not let on.

She was not just a stateswoman, and a wonderful queen,
said Alma—and "queen" in her case meant mother of the Hawaiian people—she was also a great songwriter and poet.

Really? said Yolo. He flashed on his sterile cabana-like room back at the beige hotel. It was decorated in kelly green and white. Air-conditioned, comfortable. It held no hint of queenly purple or of Hawaii's past. He could have stayed in the same hotel in Vermont.

Alma excused herself and soon came back carrying a large framed poster of Lili'uokalani. Yolo saw a large, benign colored woman's face that reminded him of his grandmother. Alma explained how the Americans had placed the queen under house arrest and threatened war if she did not resign. She gave up her throne because she knew the Hawaiian people would fight for her if she requested it and she did not want them to be killed. The people surrounded her palace, weeping, the whole night. Many Hawaiians feel the soul of the people was lost then, said Alma, with a sigh. And of course Hawaiians in the millions were dying already from the diseases the Americans had brought.

We were "annexed," she said, with bitterness. Like a small room to a large house. Yes, she added, we were, we became, the fantasy room. The place Americans went when everybody else on earth was fed up with them. The playpen. I am personally very thankful Lili'u didn't live to see the results of her noble sacrifice.

As they gazed at the picture, Alma opened another bottle of beer. Leaving the queen in his hands, she bent over the table to light another cigarette.

We Mahus Believe

WE MAHUS BELIEVE WE WERE GIVEN BY OUR AN-
cestors a very special charge. That though we are born as males,
we are to live out our lives as women. And why is this? The ma-
tronly person that everyone called "Aunty" asked.

They were sitting in a circle under a round roof made of
thatch and reeds. Below them a slight decline led toward the
narrow highway, pale as a snake, and beyond that there was
dark jade green ocean. A lusty full moon, the color of mangoes,
lit up the waves and shone into the depths. Aunty's yard was
filled with bright yellow school buses. The painter in Yolo immediately conjured a canvas and filled it completely. At the
same time, he hung on every word.

We are lucky that we are of the Polynesian world, Aunty
continued. For it is well-known that in other parts of the world,
Mahus like ourselves no longer know who they are, who they
were, or what they are supposed to be doing here on the planet
at this time. Aunty paused.

Yolo had the impression this speech was given each time the
men sat in circle. He looked around. Alma had told him about
the Mahus, but he'd found it difficult to believe they could exist.

Exist, she'd scoffed. Who do you think teaches us the hula?

And indeed it was this very same Aunty, Aunty Pearlua, who taught hula to all the young women who wanted to learn hula the right way, the way it was traditionally meant to be, and not the hula of Hollywood movies or the kind Alma had once forced herself to perform at parties.

There was a time, long time ago, Aunty Pearlua was saying, when women ruled. Well, this is not such a stretch for us because until recent times Hawaiians had a queen. Queen Lili'uokalani. But this was a time thousands of years ago when Mother rule was the dominant way of life, not only here where the original, original Hawaiians lived, but everywhere else too. The first Hawaiians were small dark people, and they were wiped out and intermingled with the tall Tahitians who, from some accounts, were pretty mean. Aunty paused and reached for her fan, which was lying on the mat beside her. We are some of both of them and more besides, so I guess we can't really complain.

This was a time so long ago as to be mythical. Our origins as Mahus, that is. But we are alive today and carrying on, so we know we are not a myth. The story goes that we were in a position to see the overthrow and enslavement of woman, and the consequent ruination of her children, which was so horrible to us that we decided that until woman was restored to her rightful place we would live her life. That is to say, we would live openly as women. That is to say, we would live openly the feminine part of our nature, which, as we know, is sometimes the dominant nature with which we are born, whether as "men" or as "women." Aunty cleared her throat and Yolo noticed the dark purple shade of her nail polish and the slight stubble visible on her chin. We also, she continued, in her rich mellow voice, made a vow to be the protector of children. That is why most Mahus that you see are teaching, feeding, or in some way, she said, with a sweep of her arm taking in the parked school buses, taking care of children. They are precious to us and we, long time ago, made a sacred vow to look out for them.

Wow, thought Yolo. All this going on in the world and some folks are just kicking back watching television.

Oh, Alma would say later when he told her about it, that's Aunty's version of the myth. She probably made it up.

But what a hip myth to make up, he thought, but did not say in light of her skepticism.

It Was the Bones

IT WAS THE BONES. ALWAYS. THAT IS WHAT THEY said. Generation after generation of their people said this to generation after generation of mine.

His name was Hugh. Kate had never met a Hugh before. How did one name a baby, defenseless, small, and new, Hugh? She thought this too might have something to do with "the generations." It did.

In the early days of moving west, clearing and claiming it, said Hugh, you could settle as much land as you could control simply by taking it from the Indians—with the help of the U.S. Cavalry—and keeping them off it. Every rancher I've talked to, if I could get him to talk about it at all, has a similar story to tell. He paused, looked at the river. Sighed.

We have rivers in the springtime, he said. In the summer they dry up or go underground.

So they're not really dry? said Kate. She liked the idea of underground rivers. She was beginning to think that human beings had underground selves, always running, limpid, clear, even when everything in the personality appeared used up, dusty, and dry.

They seem to be, said Hugh. Actually some of the first settlers died of dehydration because they thought there was no
water. The Indians would just bend over, put an ear to the
ground—and unbeknown to the settlers they'd be standing in a
dry riverbed—poke a reed in the ground, and drink. Imagine
how astonishing that must have seemed to someone from Lon-
don.

It must have been maddening, continued Hugh. They knew
every river, every stream, every rock, every tree. And they could
eat off the land too. Slugs and bugs and plants—even cactus. It
must have been really challenging starving them out.

The winter would do it, said Kate.

Right, said Hugh. Without shelter, sick, grief-stricken because so many of their people had died—then *boom*, subzero
weather. Even so, it took a while for all of them to die. They
were some of the healthiest people on earth. And to the great
surprise of everyone, in each succeeding generation, all the
way from great-grandfather Hugh Brentforth, some of them
didn't. With time it almost became a joke. There we'd be on our
considerable spread, all fenced in and secure, always around
Thanksgiving too. All of us hale and hearty and addicted to fine
brandy and snowmobiles, and then right in the middle of con-
gratulating ourselves on what a good time we're having and
how clever we and our ancestors are . . . Hugh laughed. The
area around his eyes was delicate and very pale, as if he wore
dark glasses a lot. His eyes, a green that changed to hazel in the
shifting light, were wide and blinking, as if he'd recently been
surprised.

They were sitting outside his hut at a place where the river
dropped half a dozen feet, creating a shallow waterfall. The
sound was gurgling and slow. He said it lulled him to sleep at
night.

Back before I got this sickness it didn't bother me much. It was like a ritual that happened. To tell the truth, we were all pretty used to it. You know—in Australia they still have aboriginals who go on walkabout. They go to visit what we Westerners call "sites" on the land. Places that mean a lot to them. Doesn't matter what white man's job they've been hired to do. Off they go for a while. Could be a weekend, could be a week. The land itself calls them. They hear it and go. Immediately. They drop everything. Pronto.

And do the women also go on walkabout? asked Kate. And did they in the old days just drop the mistress's brat?

Hugh laughed. I don't know. You never hear about the women roaming, but I'm sure some of them did. Probably dressed as men though because rape of aboriginal women was always as common, and as accepted, as looking at them.

They had been sitting with their legs crossed. Hugh straightened his so that his feet, blistered from the heavy rubber boots they wore most of the time, stuck out in front of him.

So there we'd be with our thirty-pound turkey and whatnot—you know, every SUV and gadget under the sun. And some old, old Indian out of nowhere would show up.

He paused.

You would have to know our ranch. It's big. So big I'm embarrassed to tell you.

Bigger than Kansas?

Almost. I'm joking, he said. But sometimes it feels that size. You can roam around it for days, never seeing a soul. A lot of the newer fencing is electric. We have guard posts.

He chuckled. Squinted at the river.

Some old Indian shows up with a plastic jug and wants water from the spring. For the bones.

Hugh rubbed together two pebbles the size of robin eggs,

loosely, in his fist. Looking at them absently he flung them into the river.

So, he continued, looking briefly at Kate, one of us tells him to wait out back until we're through with dinner. Ruined now, because of him. Though nobody wants to admit it. Ruined also of course if he didn't show up. . . . So eventually it's my turn to take him. Different Indian, you understand, but same old man. I take him in my Grand Cherokee. Which is red. We bounce along. He doesn't say a word. I make small talk—the weather, the cows—we have about six thousand. The ruts in the trail. By now we're way the hell away from the house and he just sits there with his plastic jug stuck between his knees. Everything he has on is tattered; next to him I feel conspicuously well dressed, even though I'm wearing a shirt from the Sundance catalog and an old pair of jeans.

Before we get there he tells me to stop and then he goes the rest of the way on foot. His hair is in two long braids and he's tied them with red string. I look at them as he's walking toward the spring. Try to imagine what he'd look like without them. How much less Indian. How much more like us. I figure that without them he could pass as one of America's newer immigrants.

I know the place well. Nothing there but a few cottonwood trees and a clump or two of white sage. This pitiful little spring that just keeps bubbling up no matter how dry it gets. And in Utah it can get pretty dry. I can't see him but I know he's sprinkling tobacco and praying. When I was a boy I used to sneak up behind him and watch. Then he'd reach over into the spring with the jug and take some of the water. After coming all that way, wherever it was he came from, he didn't even fill up the jug.

By the time he came back I would have finished my third or

fourth cigarette. He got in the jeep, settled the half-filled jug between his knees, and off we went. Depending on my mood I
would take him out by the main gate—where I'd lecture Harvey,
the gatekeeper, about doing a better job of things—or I'd go
back to the house and let him walk the three miles to the road.

Kate had no trouble imagining the old man. She lingered
over his braids. Was it really red string, she wondered, plaited
through them, or very frayed ribbon? She thought it was old
ribbon. The kind Indians all over the Americas—Mexico, Gua-
temala, Honduras—liked to wear.

She said, And all he said, all any of them said about the
water, was, The bones?

Yep, said Hugh. All they said. My grandmother thought the
water might be a cure for arthritis, which she had pretty bad. It
wasn't.

She tried it? asked Kate.

She tried it. Hugh smiled.

Well, years go by, said Hugh, turning slightly on his side.
The old man comes one time with his son. A sullen middle-aged
Indian and obviously a drunkard. Two Indians instead of one
made us nervous. Like maybe they were planning some kind of
attack. He laughed. I didn't care for the son nor he for me. He
looked like that Indian leader Dennis Banks only meaner.

It was always astonishing to Kate that you didn't see Indians
in America unless you looked for them. The decades of genocide
against them had left survivors with a deep fear of being seen.
No mystery either why many did pass themselves off as "newer
immigrants."

So we drove out there and the two of them walked into the
little glade where the spring was. The old man was showing it to
him, I guess. Maybe he'd been away in prison somewhere, he
had that kind of paranoid vibe. He didn't seem impressed.

When they came back he bummed a smoke. The old man had never asked for anything.

The next time the old man came he brought his grandson. The old man was almost blind and when they walked toward the spring the boy placed the old man's hand on his shoulder. I tried to imagine one of my sons or grandsons walking patiently like that with me. My grandsons play with a little gadget that looks like a handheld TV. They seem to look up from it only when it's time to eat. When they came back to the car the child looked thoughtful and as if a serious charge had been laid on him.

I told the old man about the energy development company that was going to be digging in the area. He asked when. I told him in the summer. He asked would the spring be dug into. I said yes because that's where it looked like coal deposits might be found. He asked if we could stop it. I said no.

The next year around Thanksgiving the two of them came again. I told them that what used to be a spring was now a lake. In fact, an underground lake had been found to be the source of the spring.

The old man, completely blind now, didn't seem surprised. Old Indians never seem surprised though, said Hugh. I don't know if you ever noticed that.

Kate laughed. She laughed so hard she began to cough. Hugh leaned over and patted her on the back. He looked at her quizzically.

I bet if you offered to give him his land back, she said, catching her breath, he would have looked surprised. After saying this, another wave of laughter shook her.

Hugh didn't laugh and in fact Kate could see her laughter made him sad.

He was holding his plastic jug, he continued, solemnly. A

new one, I noticed, with a stopper instead of a screw top. I was always noticing things about him, his jug, his clothes, his braids, but I never was able to notice him. There was like a fence.

We went out to the lake, which could be seen well before we came to it. At first they just sat looking at it. The boy looking, and the old man asking questions in a language I'd never heard in my life. But a language that the hills all around us and the old trees and the streams knew well. I actually had this thought. It sneaked into my consciousness. But then I squelched it. Then creakily the old man got out of the car and then the boy. And they walked toward the water.

Well, said Hugh, the lake lasted for several months. Then it dried up. The energy development folks were glad because it meant they could drill deeper with less fuss. They'd always intended to get under the lake.

The next year the old man didn't come. Neither did the boy. There was a long silence.

And I wish they had because when the digging up of the lake bed was well under way what do you think the development people discovered, not at the bottom of the lake but underneath it?

The bones? asked Kate.

Exactly, said Hugh. The bones of the old man's people from thousands of years ago. Resting there forever with a huge body of water separating them from any disturbance, and with only a tiny, trickling spring to connect them with the living.

It changed me, said Hugh. Even before I got sick.

I can see how it would, said Kate.

His devotion, he said, seeming to choke on the word.

Yes, she said.

Oh, so that's what it means to love, I thought. And had I ever loved? I thought not.

How did he, did they, even know their ancestors' bones were down there? asked Kate. And beneath a lake?

A gorgeous multilegged bug, green and gold and red, landed on Hugh's shoulder. Very carefully he removed it and studied it as he talked.

How adequate is word of mouth? How reliable is family? Kinship? How can something precious be kept that way across ten to thirty thousand years?

The old man must have felt so grateful, said Kate. To be who he was, to have had those people before him, shaping him into who he was.

Hugh was scanning the bug closely so as not to reveal the wetness of his eyes. The geologists thought, he said, that there had been a cave, a burial cave, then an earthquake, then, who knows, the ice age. . . . But they didn't really know. They made something up, you know, What the White Man Knows About Folks He's Never Known, and printed it in their journals. But they didn't inspire a lot of confidence. The old man though, he knew. And he taught what he knew to his grandson.

And did the grandson come back to the ranch?

Not yet.

Devotion, thought Kate. Hugh Brentforth V wanted to know devotion.

The more I thought about it, he said, it seemed the only thing worth knowing.

Kate lay in her hut, which was open on all sides, and quite damp from the frequent showers that, according to Armando, "never came in October," and she thought about devotion.

What was she devoted to?

To her sons, Henry and Charles, one lost to her in the

United States space program of which she knew little and feared much. Space colonies? she'd asked her son. How can you get behind anything that's colonial? The other, Charlie, an itinerant saxophone player and jazz man perpetually fulfilling the stereotype by being stoned on grass nine days out of ten. On the tenth day he looked for his supplier. Suppose something happened to one of them, she thought. What would I do? And then she thought: But it's already happened to them and there was nothing I could do. I could and did say to Henry: Be careful of joining any endeavor that is too "complicated" to tell your mother. And to Charles, since high school, I ranted, raved, and cajoled against overuse of marijuana. He'd laughed. Everybody is doing it, Mom, he'd said, as if I were the only human being on earth who was not.

She thought of Yolo. The first time she'd thought of him on this journey in a way unrelated to the stability and comfort he brought to her life. If he became sick, or say he was bitten badly by a big shark out of the novel he was reading there in Hawaii, what would she do? She'd take care of him, she knew. She could even imagine enjoying it. And surely some part of devotion was the pleasure it gave. But was this the same as loving ancestors you never saw, no one you knew had ever seen, for more than ten thousand years? But maybe these particular bones beneath Hugh Brentforth's lake had permeated the land to such a degree that the land and the lake and the spring and the souls were one.

The next day, seeing Hugh sitting with Lalika next to the deeply wrinkled and ropy trunk of a large tree that looked like, she blinked her eyes, an old Indian man, she called softly out to him:

Hey, Hugh, I've been thinking about what the old man did with the water.

In fact, she had dreamed the night before that there were

two burial grounds on Hugh's property. The ancient one from which the Indian elder got the water and a much less ancient one at the opposite edge of the land. In her dream the old man had patiently walked the perimeter of Hugh's land, holding the jug of water in his hand, until he came to a small gap at the bottom of the fence. He slid through and walked some distance into the cottonwoods. Here he stood in the center of what had been the graveyard of his tribe and of people he and his more recent ancestors had known. He knelt to pray. After praying he rose and sprinkled the water over the ground and over himself. He was trembling with exhaustion and sadness, but he was weeping with love.

In the Circle

IN THE CIRCLE WERE TWO YOUNG ABORIGINES FROM Australia. Both very dark, one with curly black hair, the other blond. Blond straight hair was natural among these very black people. Was this perhaps the reason the English settlers were so freaked out, wondered Yolo, when they came across them? What had they made of it? he wondered. They had been programmed to think all blacks were inferior. They had also been programmed to think all blonds were superior. Yolo imagined them, the British convicts and their guards, some of the most provincial folks on earth. They must have thought they'd landed on Mars.

The two men were young, in their thirties. They had come as guests of Aunty Pearlua. The shorter of the two, with the wide thoughtful "aboriginal" eyes Yolo had seen in photographs, took the talking stick, which happened to be a small shiny gourd, and turned it over and over in his hands, inspecting it carefully. After several moments, he spoke.

We are here to represent those who are coming back from the dead, he said. He gazed around the circle of men. In our country too, for many generations now, we have watched our young men die of despair. Not knowing how to stop them from hurting themselves, not knowing why they can't pull themselves out of the depression they're in; not knowing what to do to exhibit an example of life. In our country, not as rich as America and with distances more vast, there have been many cases of young men being found dead on the beach or in the outback or in the towns. Beautiful young men. Some of our best.

We ourselves, both of us, were, as younger men, addicted to petrol sniffing.

Yolo had never heard of petrol sniffing. He leaned in toward the center of the circle to hear more.

What is it to sniff petrol? asked the young man. It is to forget that once upon a time we were one with our land and with our sea. That we lived mostly on the coasts, in tropical plentitude. That we went inland into the vastness and great heat mostly on journeys of the spirit. And to keep the land company. We learned what the land and the waters loved: to be cared for, to be interacted with, to be sung to. We did not map the land as the English did, on paper, we mapped the land by singing it. There was no place unknown to us. No place that did not have its proper song. He smiled, a fondness for his ancestors suffusing his face with light. Some of our songs were so filled with what we learned from and loved about our land that they might take six months to sing.

He was quiet for a little while, turning the gourd over and over again in his hands.

What did we lose? We lost intimacy with our motherland. Mother, land, to us the same.

And so to sniff petrol is to try to avoid the anxiety of that loss. And as we exit our own time, which is now, a present we cannot bear to endure, we enter into the fake Dreamtime. Only now it is all nightmare, whether we are waking or sleeping.

Thank you, Aunty, for having us at this council. He placed the gourd back in the circle's center.

Jerry was there; it was he who had invited Yolo. Also the brother of Marshall, the young man who'd died. At the luau following Marshall's funeral Yolo had been approached as he sat in a wicker chair gazing at the moon and savoring a large plate of lau lau and a blob of pasta salad.

Howz it? asked Jerry.

Not bad, he'd replied.

Say, Jerry had said, leaning over him, his own large plate of food balanced in one hand, we think you should join us for a circle.

Me? he'd asked, looking around as if Jerry had to be referring to someone else.

Yeah, said Jerry, you. You sat with Marshall at the end. You showed up like a bradda.

But what else could I have done? Yolo thought. After all, I'm black. To be black is to know your brotherness.

He smiled at Jerry. This has been one hell of a vacation, he said.

I can imagine, said Jerry. Will you come?

Sure, Yolo had said. Will you come get me?

Where you stay? asked Jerry.

Yolo named his beige hotel.

I can sure come get you out of *dere,* man, said Jerry, laughing.

And, as good as his word, he'd showed up with his van and moved Yolo out of the hotel and into a spare room at Alma's.

We can't have you staying dere, said Jerry. What it look like, a guest of our people, coming to circle from a dead hotel? He seemed offended by the idea.

Do you mind? he'd asked Alma. But she'd looked at him

like he was crazy and flung open the door to a small, airy room painted white with lots of Hawaiian art, including the large framed poster of the queen, on the walls. She was as usual drinking a beer and the smoke from her cigarette lingered in his hair.

The man with blond hair took the gourd. He must get stared at a lot, thought Yolo. Most folks would assume he straightened and dyed his hair, like James Brown used to do when he was "James Brown and the Famous Flames." Brown's group had dyed their hair an outrageous reddish orange and against their very dark skin, almost as black as the aborigine's, the color of their hair had expressed excitement itself.

We have tried everything, the young man was saying. Lecturing. Cajoling. Loving. Hating. But we have not been able to prevent the young from seeing the truth. That they have lost the future. Some might dispute this statement, and that is their prerogative. I'm saying this is what it looks like to the youths who sniff petrol. There they are, poor, discarded by the society that has slaughtered their people and taken their land; they might be fourteen thousand miles from the nearest disco. A bottle of petrol is the closest they will get to a plane ticket. The closest they will get to leaving their barren environment.

He paused. Studied the gourd.

I too used to feel that way. It is a miracle I am still alive. He stopped talking and sat reflecting for several minutes; everyone in the circle remained respectful and still. He continued: My older sister, who had gone away to find work in the city, came back for me. We lived in one room at the back of her employer's house. She said only one thing: I don't want you to watch the master of the house, my employer. I want you to watch me, your sister.

And that is all she said to me for months. We lived in silence.

She worked, hard and long. She fed us, kept us clothed and clean. She drew her strength from a small circle of Nunga women similarly situated in the city, far from their folks. At first I missed my visions of freedom, the weightless pleasure of abandoning myself. I also wanted to talk, to dribble at the mouth with words as I had done on petrol. But she was like a stone.

I watched her face, broad and flat and black, as aboriginal faces are described so often in literature, and I saw how tired she was. This frightened me. For it made me think how useless her struggle was. How impossible and absurd. To try to have a life in a place your life was considered worthless. To my shame, I used to laugh at her. But it was my fear that was laughing. And she did not even look at me. She would not respond. Each day she got up off her mat on the floor, made tea for us. Left me two slices of bread. And went out to serve bread with jam, coffee with cream, bacon with eggs, to the owners of the big house that we saw no matter where we looked, standing or lying in our own small room, and that in fact blocked the sun.

When her employers and their children saw me they related to me as to an oddity. My blond hair might have gotten me points, but I remembered what my sister had said. I was not to watch them. No matter with what curiosity they watched me, I was to watch her. I understood that the fulfillment of this requirement was my share of the food, the rent. It was also my education.

For what did I see? My sister's devotion, saving me, showed me myself. Someone worth saving, someone, in the female form that was my sister, who would save himself.

He paused.

There was no God involved, he ended thoughtfully, though the evangelicals have arrived in Australia with the same force they've arrived among the oppressed all over the globe. My sister embodied all that we thought lost. She had become the land, the sea, the freedom of the Dreamtime. Her behavior said: Though we have been taken from Her, yet I am Her.

He glanced around the circle, embracing everyone with his eyes. He looked at his friend. An impish look passed between them.

We're off petrol, he said, smiling. But now we're both inactive without coffee.

Everyone in the circle laughed.

Toward the
Middle of Their Stay

TOWARD THE MIDDLE OF THEIR STAY IN THE JUN-
gle Armando and Cosmi invited them to dinner in the com-
pound in which they'd received their very first meal. It was the
place the two of them stayed. There was a handsome thatched
dining area with a rough-hewn wooden table, a stove made out
of stones and cement, and, in the corner of the ceiling nearest
the huge trees that stood outside, there was a large iguana. This
thick-waisted creature with its glittering eyes watched every
move they made and caused everyone at the table to think of the
varied critters they were sharing quarters with. Every hut, it
turned out, had its nonhuman resident.

I have an iguana too, said Missy, only thank God it's smaller
than Godzilla there.

And does it watch your every move? asked Lalika.

I don't think so, said Missy. It seems mostly to sleep.

This one thinks we're television, said Rick, making a face
at it.

Rick had been having the most trouble, Kate thought, of
everyone. He could not let himself enter the world of Grandmother. He was fighting it tooth and nail. Instead of submitting,

finding the "brick" or "scale of the serpent" that opened like a door into the experience, Rick turned aside. Turning aside at the crucial moment meant he was left in a kind of limbo. Laughing, crying, jumping around, disturbing everybody else's trip.

What creature lives in your house? Kate asked him.

He thought. Moths, he said finally. Lots of moths as large as bats.

Wow, said Hugh. And they don't bother you?

He shrugged: According to Carlos Casteneda, Don Juan said that moths are the ancestors.

Really, said Missy. But if they're big as bats I don't know if I'd want to see them.

There's no choosing of who or what visits you when you come here, said Armando. It is only important that something does.

A gecko seems to be the only thing in my *tambo,* said Kate. But every time I say something or think something with any degree of certitude it makes that weird gecko sound.

It is agreeing, said Armando. Geckos always do that. You will notice that when you tell a lie or try to evade an issue it will not second you.

Everyone turned to Hugh.

I have not one bat but a family of them, he said. I just close myself up in my mosquito netting at night and hope their teeth are not sharp.

These are the creatures in whose homes you are living, said Armando. Think how patient they are with you.

During the second half of your visit notice who comes to visit you. By the way, he asked, has anyone been disturbed by the jaguar sounds?

I wasn't so disturbed by the screeching right outside my hut, said Hugh, but I did lose some sleep listening to the men trying to chase it away. They were crashing through the jungle like a bunch of elephants.

Armando laughed. Usually a jaguar is a good thing, but sometimes it is the spirit of a sorcerer who is up to no good. That is why it was chased out. We did not send for it.

Where did you find chicken? asked Lalika, who was beginning to sleep so soundly that she heard nothing. Gingerly she lifted her spoon to her mouth and blew on the steaming broth.

Is there such a thing as jungle hen? asked Rick, seriously. He was studying his bowl, which was made of wood, and inhaling the aroma of the broth before drinking it.

There is a small farm not very far from here, said Armando. The woman raises chickens to eat and to sell. We brought chickens into the forest with us, only you did not see them.

Were they in a separate boat? asked Kate.

Yes, said Armando. They came in the boat that also brought the *platanos* and the grains.

The banana and quinoa diet is getting a little boring, said Missy.

That is why tonight we have broth, said Armando. But tomorrow, just like always, our one meal of the day will be one boiled *platano* and one bowl of grain. If you are tired of quinoa you can have rice or millet or oatmeal.

Missy made a face.

We will all be so slim, said Kate. We will be like Bette Midler in *Ruthless People*.

Oh, I loved that movie! said Missy.

You are all talking a bit too much, said Armando, who had cautioned them from the beginning to stay out of popular culture and in their own interior worlds.

When you are caught up in the world that you did not design as support for your life and the life of earth and people, it is like being caught in someone else's dream or nightmare. Many people exist in their lives in this way. I say exist because it is not really living. It is akin to being suspended in a dream one is having at night, a dream over which one has no control. You are going here and there, seeing this and that person; you do not know or care about them usually, they are just there, on your interior screen. Humankind will not survive if we continue in this way, most of us living lives in which our own life is not the center. You would not drive a car looking out the side window, would you? Yet that is what it has come to for many human beings; they are driving their lives forward while watching what is happening along the road or even in the rearview mirror.

So on this retreat with Grandmother, not only will we observe as much silence as possible, we will also spend our time in connection with our interior world.

I find I am talking with everyone, Kate said to Armando when he visited her after the light, delicious meal. Is it a problem?

Armando had brought her a pitcher of green water in which to wash herself. It was purified water in which leaves of a plant had been crushed. She was to pour it over herself, from head to toe. The bits of leaves were to be left on her skin to dry. Armando explained to her the reason shamans knew which plants were good to use to help people heal. It is simple, he said, the plants themselves tell us. Either in dreams, or in meditation or by accident. He laughed. Sometimes you will find yourself chewing something, a leaf or plant stem you picked up in the forest, that makes you feel so much better!

This will cleanse your skin so deeply you will feel your pores breathing, he said. You will breathe with the forest. Actually all of the body was meant to breathe, naked, with the environment, he added. Not just the face.

I do not think it is a problem if you talk with everyone, he added, after showing her how to rub the medicine over her skin. Do you realize that in every group there will be one person who is afraid to go to Grandmother and one person Grandmother does not want to talk to anymore? She does not need to tell you anything more. She has told you everything you need to know. What you need to do now is listen. To accept. I have observed you with the others; they seem to talk far more than you. I think it is okay, he said. We never are sure how the *medicina* is going to work. What it will call forth. If you maintain respect for the *medicina* and for the sacred space of healing and also for the story you are hearing, all will be well.

His Streaked Reddish Hair

HIS STREAKED REDDISH HAIR WAS BEGINNING TO reveal dark roots.

Each morning before sitting in circle Rick jogged through the jungle to a wide place in the river, ripped the towel from around his neck, his only attire, and plunged in.

Aren't you afraid? they asked.

Nah, he said, I've been swimming with piranhas all my life. I just didn't know it. He laughed. He had a ragged, feral look when he laughed because his teeth, polished to a high gloss, were uneven. A wispy mustache in which there were glints of gray belied his youthful look. Even in repose he appeared tense and driven.

After Kate had "seen" him he began to unwind, rather quickly, to her mind. And yet, when she spoke of this to Armando he reminded her it was the yagé. And that she, Kate, had needed to be present in the circle, alert, in order to do this particular dance that Grandmother required.

He laughed. I was getting a bit weary of Mr. Young Man Let Me Stay.

What do you mean? asked Kate.

He wants to stay young forever, said Armando. Like a

Dracula or like these bats we have sometimes in the jungle. They drink so much blood! From animals, from people. And only because they have a fight with old age and with death, which of course will win. He shrugged. Mr. Young Man Let Me Stay, he said again, and chuckled. Grandmother has a message for him.

I don't know how long it took me to realize my family's wealth came from the sale of narcotics to black people, but I think it was a long time, he said one day as Kate and Lalika crowded into Lalika's hammock for the afternoon siesta. Because the hammock was narrow they couldn't actually lie down; they sat facing each other, their legs touching. Rick sat near them on a mat on the floor.

Kate and Lalika had taken a liking to Rick, who had bought a charango made of armadillo hide and sometimes in the afternoons attempted to play it. He had no musical talent whatsoever, which amused them. He had surprised them by saying their liking him was both predictable and uncanny. Puzzled, they had teased him and played with him and pursued the hidden thread that connected them to this rather scrawny, bespeckled, youthful-appearing man.

Black people always like us, he said, and that is why, in my opinion, it was easy to sell dope to them. My uncles have told me that they always had black friends, but after a while it was as if they didn't know what to do with them. They were in America, not in Italy. They didn't know how to do hospitality to strangers as they might have done at home. And at that point I think they remembered where to draw the line. That in fact there was a line. They could sell drugs to blacks but they were not themselves to be hooked on the stuff because if they became hooked on the stuff they couldn't move up in American society and moving up in American society was what they wanted the most. After such a long sentence Rick let out a breath. To be respectable, he added.

So they hooked their black friends?

The friends were willing, said Rick. At least at first. Only later did they realize they had to hook others in their communities, they couldn't push drugs to white people, in order to stay medicated.

I've never understood it, said Kate, to be medicated on drugs, heroin or cocaine or whatever, what is the appeal? Do people just want to get high, fly away from their troubles? Are they trying to knock themselves out? What?

Rick was thoughtful for a moment. They just want to feel normal, he said. The way they used to feel. They can still remember that feeling, you know, like a sense of home within, and they keep trying to get back to it.

I certainly understand that, said Lalika. Sometimes I feel like if I can't get back to the wholeness of myself I'd rather be dead. I feel like being dead might even approximate that feeling, you know, of being at one with myself again, of being whole.

Kate took one of her feet and began to massage it.

Umm, said Lalika.

Kate chuckled. If you're dead you can't feel massage.

It's true that some people, especially on cocaine, like to feel powerful and smart, if only for a few minutes or a couple of hours. Rick laughed. But that's because for a moment sometime in their lives they felt this way naturally, and subsequently lost it. That feeling of being powerful and smart they had, maybe after winning a spelling bee in third grade, is the most "normal" and "at home" in themselves they've ever felt. They long to have it again.

There had been only two sessions with Grandmother left.
During the circle before, Rick had acted out as usual, pretending to be an orangutan, grunting and rutting around the floor.
Everyone else was quiet, immersed in their own journeys. Kate
sat as usual completely still, as though she had also taken the
medicine. Her eyes were open though. She watched as Rick
rose from his seat, a low-slung, rope-backed, wooden chair like
all the others, and, after studying it for a moment, deliberately
turned it over. He then proceeded to sit on the floor and to attempt to sprinkle dust from the floor over his head. There was
little of this because the earthen floor was covered with a thick
straw carpet. He kept his right arm looped over his head, however, which gave him a distinctly simian look. Only it wasn't
amusing. He was disturbing the other participants who, distracted by the noise and movement of Rick, began to squirm in
their seats. Armando and Cosmi tried during each session to
work with Rick, to ease him along on his journey, a journey it
was clear he was afraid to make. They did not wish to exclude
him from the circle because, as they had explained to the group,
what makes a circle sacred is that those who show up for it are
the ones who belong in it. Casting anyone out, no matter how
bizarre their behavior, drained the energy of the circle. However, Kate could see they were getting fed up with Rick. After
singing to him and blowing smoke over him and finally sprinkling him with *agua florida,* Armando strode away in disgust.
Rick was now starting to drool and to make motions that suggested other forms of regression.

Kate closed her eyes for a moment and let the image of Rick
as he was crawling around on the floor before her merge with
the cool, tense, intellectual Rick who always seemed to have

control of himself. What she saw was an empty space. Rick was invisible. Or at least he thought he was.

When she opened her eyes he was on his knees, like a two-year-old, right in front of her. He was looking at her with a look that dared her to do something. Instinctively, she knew what it was.

Looking him directly in the eye she had said to him, enunciating very clearly: *I see you.*

A shock went through his body, and the selves or pieces of selves that had internally been lying all over the floor coalesced.

She repeated: *I see you.*

He made one last crawling turn around the floor as if to escape the radar of her gaze, but the circle was very small and eventually he was right in front of her again.

I still see you, she said.

Rick stood up, looked self-consciously around the circle, and departed. He was gone all the next day.

It was my father who Anglicized our name, he said. *Richards,* he said, when he thoughtfully and quietly joined them again.

What was it before? asked Kate.

I'm embarrassed to tell you, he said. Not Corleone.

Oh, I remember them, said Lalika. Those people in *The Godfather.* They thought selling dope to black people didn't matter because we're animals.

There was silence. Kate took Lalika's other foot and tugged at her toes.

I have a friend who had a heart attack from crack, Lalika continued. She said crack kept her from remembering.

Saartjie? Kate asked.

There was a long silence, as Kate stroked the sides of Lalika's foot.

Yes, said Lalika, sighing. I told her to try to hold on, to remember Saint Saartjie. She paused. The people who got us out
of jail kept wanting us to tell our story. So we could raise money
to pay for the huge legal expense. We must have told it to a
couple of hundred different groups and to television and the
newspapers. How the policeman tried to rape us both. How I
defended Gloria. How they beat us, locked us up. Raped us over
and over, jailers and inmates alike. Filmed everything. Sold the
film all over the world, as far as we knew. The sadness on her
beautiful face made tears come to Kate's eyes. Saint Saartjie disappeared and just the regular old Saartjie, dragged around for
folks to look at and poke fun at, was left. She couldn't stand it,
Gloria said.

How did you?

I could still see Saint Saartjie in her even though she couldn't
see Her in herself. I felt like I was doing something to help all the
Saartjies in the world. Lalika thought for a moment. Maybe it's
because I had a grandmother once. One time when I was very
small, I remember I was living with a very old lady and they told
me she was my grandmother. And even though she was old and
sick and soon died she seemed to give me a strong shot of something.

Love? asked Rick.

People didn't talk about love so much. I guess I would call
what she gave me a real strong hit of *being thereness*.

Presence? asked Kate.

Yeah. As long as she was around there was no such thing as
being alone.

We lived in the whitest possible town while I was growing
up, said Rick. With an English name to fit ours. In fact, it was a

little bit of England, even eighteenth-century England, right on the coast of North America. Black people were not even welcome there to work.

Well, Kate said teasingly, you did your part. You dyed your hair red.

It just seemed to go with the landscape, said Rick. And with my mother's carefully chosen and maintained ash-blond locks. It wasn't supposed to be red, of course, but like so many things I got it wrong.

How did you find out? asked Lalika.

A predictable story, he said: Having gone to lily-white schools practically from birth, in which Jews, black people, and Italians were not present, at least not as themselves, I lucked out and went off to a college that had everybody. My roommate was a black guy. When I brought him home for a weekend I realized my parents were far too nice to him. So nice he would have had to be crazy ever to go back.

What niceness was this? asked Kate.

The totally phony kind, said Rick. The kind that said you're such a different expression of life we will suffocate you with our overreaching acceptance.

I didn't understand it. But then I started to date a woman of color. And they freaked. They started to tell me stuff about black people I'd never heard before. They seemed to know an awful lot about the drugs they used. And the crimes they committed while on them. They warned me not to go into their neighborhoods. This was shocking. I had no idea either of them knew anything about black neighborhoods.

And then I met one of my uncles who had not changed his name. I moved in with him, after running off from home. Under prodding and after teasing me about my hair, which was where I've always carried on any rebellion I felt, he said enough to start me to think. He introduced me to another uncle, and to cousins I didn't know I had. Selling drugs to oppressed people was our family business, for generations. My family had sold the stuff for years, before they owned the hotels and restaurants, office buildings and elected officials, that I was familiar with. I started to understand why my hair would always be dark at the roots. Just as the Kennedys would always have those Joseph Kennedy teeth. I started to understand why to myself and often to other people I have felt invisible.

After the Last Circle

AFTER THE LAST CIRCLE, MISSY PROCLAIMED A breakthrough. During the first sessions, Armando and Cosmi had spent considerable time with her. Patiently encouraging her to get out of the way of herself. It was clear to Kate, sitting across the room from Missy, that she had every intention of being healed, but lacked the courage to let it happen. Her body grew as tight as a ripe tomato, and every orifice seemed closed: eyes, mouth, ears. She crossed her legs and became rigid. Nothing is coming into me, she seemed to say, and nothing is going out.

The more Armando sang—songs so lovely they made Kate weep—and the more Cosmi played his reed flute, the more Missy dug in her heels. Once in a while tears would leak from beneath her lashes and that would be enough encouragement for Armando and Cosmi to hover over her minutes longer.

Armando had told them all many times: It is hard to believe, but there is something inside of you, no matter how sick and fed up with your sickness you are, that does not want you to heal. It will actually fight you. Sometimes I think of it as a small boy, he said, and laughed. He is there having a good time at your expense and if you get well he worries there will be nothing left to do. No games to play with your sick body, no games to play with your mind. And this little boy will have to be *negotiated*. It was one of Armando's favorite words. He will have to be *negotiated*, just like you would talk to a lawyer. If I am well, you must tell him, there will actually be lots more for you to do. More games for you to play, because we will be much stronger. If we are much stronger, we can go more places. We can have more fun. He is an odd little boy, this part of yourself that wants to control you while you are sick. And sometimes we are all charmed by him. That is why sometimes people who are not very sick will suddenly die. They have listened to his voice too long. It is very seductive.

One afternoon, as Armando was singing over her and Cosmi was fanning her with his fan, Missy seemed to die. Her rigid body became flaccid. Her head lolled to one side. Kate moved immediately to sit beside her, and when Missy woke up, Kate was looking down at her. Missy said: Oh, something's gone.

Whew, said Kate. We thought you were.

Missy sat up, looked around at the circle, and seemed to realize where she was.

I've been away, she said.

Welcome back, said Kate.

You have to understand that my grandfather, who incested me, was very small, she told them the next day. He was tiny for a man. And I think that had something to do with it. He was also a clown. That's what he did professionally. He was the clown, especially at children's parties. He was also the clown very often at home. My mom and I lived with him, because my father went off to the army and never came back. If he died there she never told me. She used to tell me God was my father and that that made me and Jesus siblings. I loved Jesus! Even today I think Jesus is really the coolest. And talk about hair. I thought it was just Cool City that his locks were always long. The only other person I knew who dared wear strange hair was my grandfather, so he was always right up there with Jesus Christ in my mind.

My grandfather, Timmy Wimmins, took care of us, and, while she worked, he took care of his little Squiggly Wiggly. Me. My mother didn't find out what was going on until I was ten, when I was trying to stop playing with Timmy Wimmins and she wondered what had gotten into me.

Well, she said, frowning, when she found out what had literally gotten into me, she was not amused.

We left my grandfather's house. But we couldn't leave off feeling love for him. Except for what he'd done to me, he was the greatest guy.

Missy looked down into the river. It was swollen from a thunderstorm the night before. The glints of light across it matched the highlights in her brown hair.

I missed him terribly, she said. And so did my mom. We were so used to him. To his jokes, to his pranks, to his dependability. I was used to him physically too, she added thoughtfully. I didn't want him messing around my private parts anymore, she said primly, but I sure missed snuggling and cuddling and lying on the sofa on a rainy afternoon watching cartoons. And eating popcorn with walnuts and raisins!

My mom missed having him cook for us. Missed having him waiting at the door with a glass of wine in his hand for her. Missed never having to take the car to the repair shop or to get it washed.

She paused. In a way, my grandfather was our father and our husband.

The five of them were sitting together watching the river.

And did he incest her? asked Hugh.

I don't think so, said Missy. But we never talked about it. He might have, when she was small.

I outgrew him, actually. At ten I was taller than he was.

They were silent for a while.

He used to tickle me. Make me laugh. He was so funny. He'd be wearing his clown clothes and his clown nose. And then the playing would run off into sex; but it was still like playing. He'd started playing with me so early I never knew there was a cutoff point. I was actually waiting for the tingle.

Kate laughed. The tingle?

Yes, said Missy. And if I tingled really well and enjoyed it a lot, he was so pleased.

Like after going to the bathroom by yourself when you're little, said Lalika.

Exactly, said Missy. I think he thought good sex could be trained, like potty training. But when I understood what we'd done was wrong I was afraid to let myself tingle anymore. I couldn't with boyfriends, I couldn't with the man I married. It just felt like the wrong thing to do.

How did I learn it was wrong? I'm not sure I remember. It just started to feel wrong. And I noticed none of my friends ever talked about any tingling.

I couldn't express to anyone, especially not my mother, how much I had enjoyed playing. Even in therapy I had the feeling of being perverse.

What happened to your grandfather? asked Rick.

He died, said Missy. He couldn't be a clown anymore because his heart wasn't in it. He missed us. I used to wake up at night crying thinking how much he must be missing us. We were his reason for living.

And yet, said Hugh, he took advantage of you. You were a child.

I was an infant when it started. Missy bowed her head.

I had such a hard time figuring it out. I took to marijuana like a duck to water. Always high. Then I switched to every other pill or potion you can name. Cocaine made me think I was smart enough to cope, but it was so expensive and my nose started to collapse.

Wow, said Kate.

But, said Missy, Grandmother told me to come and sit by the river. I sat here for most of the morning and part of the afternoon, looking at the water. What I see is that it has everything in it and it just keeps flowing. And look what else happened, she said, looking at them, you all have drifted down to the river to be with me. I promised myself, sitting here, that the first person who disturbed my solitude I would open to. That opening beyond where I was afraid to go would be the medicine for my cure.

Are we the first people you've told?

The scary parts? Yes.

Lalika took one of Missy's hands. Kate took the other. Hugh and Rick placed their hands on her knees. Ah, said Armando, coming up behind them. Are we praying?

Yes, they said simply, inviting him and Cosmi, who walked behind him, to join them.

After ten minutes Missy opened her eyes wide, looked around at all of them, and asked: Did anybody else see dragons?

Gosh, I'm glad you asked, said Rick. When I finally let go I saw a dragon like the one in *Way of the Shaman*. I was reading it on the way down here; I think that might have had something to do with it.

I don't think so, said Hugh. I haven't read it yet, although I intend to as soon as I get home. I saw *humongous* dragons. Breathing fire.

Well, said Rick, mine breathed fire for a while and then water for a while, and then people. Streams of people just poured out of its mouth. He was thoughtful for a moment. We were being vomited up, our species, out of the depths of our own unconscious, is what it felt like.

Gee, said Missy.

Yeah, said Rick. And at that point, seeing all of humanity aimed at my head, I gratefully died.

It felt like I died, said Hugh. And I was afraid, right up until it happened. I had this feeling of foolishness too. Like, whatever possessed me to leave my cozy home in the good ole US of A to come to this godforsaken wilderness and drink this foul-tasting stuff handed to me by Indians who really should be giving me hemlock, if they knew what my people had done to them? But then when I actually started dying, I saw it wasn't so bad. He lay back from the circle, his hands under his head, and looked at the sky. Being dead is profoundly peaceful, he said.

Well, said Missy, everybody told me I'd see dragons. But I just saw really big snakes. A couple of them, she added. Wrapped around each other.

But aren't dragons snakes that get out of hand? asked Rick.

The creature I entered was so huge, said Kate, I couldn't even tell it was a snake. Or a dragon. It looked like the side of a building. Except it was jeweled. Or beaded. I wonder if ancient people learned beadwork from their experience with this being's skin. It was of breathtaking beauty. Anyhow, I lifted a flap, almost like opening a window, a beaded or jeweled window, and slid in.

And were you afraid? asked Missy.

I'd come so far, said Kate. Fear seemed beside the point. I

guess I doubted I'd have much of an experience. And then, after a very full experience with Grandmother, she drifted away.

Really, said Lalika.

Yes, said Kate, that is why I stopped taking the medicine with you. By my third session with Grandmother the snakes or dragons or whatever they were were so small I could hold them in my hands. They were white and blue, and playful, like cartoon figures.

You have now experienced what humans thousands of years ago, to their great amazement I'm sure, also experienced. Such a long time ago we cannot truly imagine it. It is what humans have been experiencing for thousands of years since. Grandmother Yagé is a medicine of origins and endings, yes, Armando concluded, softly. That is why Grandfather reptile always appears.

A Person Is Visible

A PERSON IS VISIBLE ONLY WHEN IT IS POSSIBLE to perceive what sustains him, said Armando to Rick. His nourishment, so to speak. Your nourishment—the food you ate, the education you received, the trips you took, the houses you bought, and the clothes, even the shoes, you bought—was kept secret. Your parents did not tell you that your shiny teeth were paid for by those that fell from the gums of drug addicts.

They thought to protect you from the suffering of the world by making sure you did not know about it. Yet it was the suffering of the world that was feeding you.

Their teeth fall out? asked Rick.

Yes, said Armando. The drug addict does not always care to eat. Or to brush. Flossing is out of the question.

You are very thin, he continued. But not invisible altogether. He paused, seeming to wait for Rick's response.

Rick looked down at his hands and then away from them toward the river.

I'm thin because I binge, he said, on all the food I can possibly stuff into my body, and then I purge.

So, said Armando after a moment, you are an old hand at throwing up.

Yes, said Rick. Even before I knew the family secret. I felt instinctively that we had too much of everything: food, clothes, money. And my parents, especially my father, was always urging me to take more. Eat! Drink! Buy! That was the only time he sounded Italian. Even *Roman*. Even *imperial*. He laughed. Yes, he continued, chuckling, he looked just like those Roman emperors in the movies, setting off to conquer, to eat up, the earth. Devouring everything seems to be in our genes.

And then when I knew . . . I didn't know what to feel. I realized I felt nothing. And my life went on as always. Nothing changed, even though I now knew something so shocking about my family, our history, and myself; people still treated me as if I were special. Our driver still tipped his hat when he opened the door of the car for me.

But then, one day, I noticed he wasn't really looking at me—to see me—when he did it. I saw it was my overcoat and hat, my well-polished boots and tailored suit, he recognized. Who I was myself he had no clue and didn't care about it either. I could have been a mannequin. A blow-up doll, he said, and laughed.

Seriously, he said to Armando, since coming to America all of us "ethnics" who could pass for white people did so. We dropped as much as we could of whatever heart, soul, or rhythm made us unique. It's curious now that everywhere you look there are white men, but in my view most of them are invisible. We don't look at each other, you know. Not anymore. We're afraid someone will have the poor taste to ask: What is your power source?

And certainly you don't want ethnic studies taught in school, said Kate, because that is exactly the question that is asked.

When a foreigner from a poor country visits America, said Armando, he feels he is moving among shadows. Shadows with teeth! He laughed. Not even the shadows of nature. We have not known why this is so. Because in movies from America that we have seen the white man's face has filled the entire screen. His troubles have seemed real enough to make him more like us. We see he has suffered. But when we get here, he is so stiff! Besides, though we have seen so much of white men, they do not appear to see us.

They dare not, said Rick, shrugging. Any dark-skinned or poor person is likely to be from a place we have harmed.

The more powerful the powerful appear the more invisible they become, said Armando. This used to work differently than now. In the old days it was said that the powerful merged with the divine and the divine was all that one saw. But now the powerful have merged with the shadow, really with death, and when you encounter them they are really hard to see. Even for a shaman. Sometimes one thinks: There is a woman who sleeps with this invisible person, every night. Of what does she dream?

What is the medicine for this invisibility that white men have? asked Rick. An invisibility they are spreading to others.

Armando looked for a long time in the direction of the river, and yet his gaze seemed to hover just above it, at the edge of the trees.

In my opinion, he said, after a while, the only medicine that cures invisibility among the powerful is tears.

There was a long silence. Eventually Armando continued. Think of your presidents, he said. And how you only learned to see them, truly see them, after they died. Because then much of their true nourishment could at least be hinted at. Think of how they looked on television as they calmly ended the lives of nations and people, small children, rivers, donkeys, and goats.

He paused.

It would have been better for everyone if, instead of calmness, they gave their orders weeping.

Crocodile tears, said Rick, with a snort.

Perhaps, said Armando. Besides, they were not hired by the people who control them to feel. Only to do.

I don't feel, said Rick. Or, I feel only enough to get by. I married the woman of color I dated in college, and she did the feeling for both of us.

And sleeping beside you, said Armando, of what did she dream?

That I could not possibly be so unfeeling. It was so odd to her she never believed it. She thought something, some horror story, some experience of sadness, would shake me to my core and that in that core would be just what you are speaking of, a bucket of tears. It's never happened.

Are you so attached to your toys? asked Armando. You are a rich man, no?

Very rich. I have the money that should have built hospitals, should have built schools. Should have fed and educated generations of children who ended up in prison. My wife used to remind me of this, before she bailed out.

And? said Armando.

Nothing, said Rick. I have lots of stuff but basically I live in one room.

Does it face the water? asked Armando.

It does, said Rick, surprised.

All your tears are calling you, said Armando, touching his knee.

You Must Live:
A Future Consequence

YOU MUST LIVE FOR AT LEAST TWO YEARS IN SPACE, SAID Grandmother. *It will take at least that long to make you positive that space is where you have always lived. There are people who think they must travel through the air to reach space, but that is because they do not understand. You are born into space, out of space, space is your home forever. Earth is like a dust mote in the cosmos. An interesting, even fascinating, dust mote. But a dust mote. It is like a raft on a river and the river is space.*

She told me I must live in space for two years, Kate said to Yolo. I don't understand that at all. How am I going to do that?

Yolo smiled at her. Grandmother has a sense of humor, he said.

The next time she returned from a trip she thought she'd been brought to the wrong address. Opening her gate, blinking in surprise, she saw that Yolo had painted her house sky blue.

It's the color you felt at home in, in my canvases, he said.

Yes, she said, enchanted.

Kate Awoke the Last Day

KATE AWOKE THE LAST DAY OF THE RETREAT EAGER
to go home. Packing her things, saying good-bye to the little hut
that had been her nest, she remembered a dream of the night before. She had been visited by a very old woman famous for making things beautiful. She'd swept into Kate's drab abode and,
just by thinking it, transformed each room into a bouquet of
flowers. They were still rooms, but when she touched them, the
walls turned into flowers. Kate had walked through her now
very spacious, long, flower-walled house, a house that breathed
perfume and freshness, toward the beach where she could see
the Old One walking. She was wearing something that she said
was made of vinyl, and therefore she could not walk directly in
the sunlight, and she and her respectful assistant turned more
toward the shadows as Kate approached them begging the old
woman to stay. Kate felt a longing for her continued presence
that she knew was aroused in people wherever the old woman
went. *Please stay,* she cried, but the old woman was already
telling the assistant about the next job she had on her schedule,
the next drab abode that awaited her magic visit. So that is old
age! Kate thought, waking. The ability to visit what is ugly and
to transform into beauty anything you touch.

In the boat she told the dream to Armando, who smiled at her.

I did not know you were concerned about old age, he said.

I didn't know it either, said Kate. But I guess I was.

She reminds me of my grandmother, said Lalika.

Her shaved head was purple where it appeared beneath her white crocheted cap. Her eyes were serene and clear.

There was a closeness among them, Missy, Kate, Rick, La-lika, Hugh, Armando, and Cosmi, that felt very ancient and very sweet. They were all considerably slimmer too.

For a long time the boat hummed along, skirting the jungle, and only after many hours did the inhabitants of villages begin to appear. Small clear-cut farms with a couple of scrawny mules and a dozen or so chickens or perhaps a goat. Thatched huts slightly larger than the ones they had left. It was like entering another world. Everything, after the opulence of the forest, seemed battered and sickly. The people, the women especially, looked shockingly oppressed, dejected, and malnourished as they dragged themselves about their hard-packed yards, so re-cently the lush floor of the rapidly disappearing Amazon forest. It seemed to Kate that every young woman they saw, above the age of thirteen, was pregnant. Near one of these farms the boat stopped for a woman dressed in clean but frayed and tattered clothes. They made room for her in the boat, but for the rest of the trip, two and a half hours or so, she kept herself away from them. It was as if she feared they would think her unfit to share the boat with them.

When they arrived safely at the outpost where a car awaited them Kate was relieved. Because they were hungry they stopped to eat at a restaurant that served rice and beans and fish, but no vegetables.

The farmer in her awoke. Surely people could grow some

kind of greens here, she said to Armando. In all this heat and humidity. She was thinking especially of collards and kale, which did so well in the semitropical climate of the American South. And tomatoes, beans, and squash!

He shrugged, gratefully took his plate, and ate hungrily, as they all did, savoring their first nonretreat meal. There were small pebbles in the beans that almost cost Kate a tooth, but she carefully ate around them.

At the airport they exchanged phone numbers and e-mail addresses and hugged and kissed one another good-bye. This is the way people live now, thought Kate. If you're lucky you get to spend intense weeks or months with people with whom you exchange the most intimate and vital information; then, you take off again, you are gone. She wondered if they would ever see one another again. She hoped so, but did not expect it to happen.

Yolo Woke

YOLO WOKE IN ALMA'S HOUSE THINKING OF ALMA'S health. She must weigh two hundred pounds, at least, he thought. And her smoking and drinking is nonstop. He did not see how he could say this to her, however. He remembered her fierce temper. She'd probably kick him out before he had a chance to pack.

As he was thinking this, she stuck her head in the doorway. Want coffee? she asked.

Did he want coffee? He sure did.

No, thank you, he said.

At breakfast he asked for hot water, into which he squeezed a lemon.

That looks healthy, she said. For breakfast she was having hash-brown potatoes, rice, sausage, ham, eggs, toast and jam, and a big cup of Folgers with whipped cream.

You were gone almost all night, she said, offering her best James Dean squint through cigarette smoke that briefly obliterated her face. What was Aunty Pearlua up to?

Yolo laughed. She's something, he said. Is Pearlua her real name? he asked.

I doubt it, said Alma, waiting.

The surprise guest was none other than your namesake, he said, taking a slice of mango from a platter Alma ignored. Many Hawaiians disliked mangoes, he'd been told. They'd eaten too many as children, when times were tight.

Alma took a forkful of eggs and sausage. You mean you were not the surprise guest?

Everybody was a surprise, really, he said.

I didn't even know my namesake was still alive, she said.

Very much so, said Yolo.

What's she doing with herself?

What was she doing with herself the last time you checked in? he asked.

Some kind of diet thing, I think, said Alma, taking a bite of butter-slathered toast.

Did you know Aunty Pearlua and Aunty Alma are related? asked Yolo.

Everybody around here is related, said Alma. That's what it means to be on islands thousands of miles from anybody else.

So Yolo began to tell her about his evening.

One of these days I hope you meet Kate, he began. The experience I had last night is the only kind she's interested in. I never dreamed it could happen to me.

Alma raised an eyebrow while lighting a cigarette.

Being with the people of the world in a certain way, he elaborated, noting her look. A way that erases all boundaries and bullshit.

He told her how Jerry had invited him, because he'd sat beside the body of her son Marshall on the beach.

Well, said Alma, he didn't invite me. There was bitterness in the smoke she blew across the table at him.

Yolo shrugged. We were all men, he said, until Aunty Alma came.

Aunty Pearlua and them would be highly insulted by that re-
mark, said Alma.

Oops, said Yolo. You know what I mean.

Yes, I do know, said Alma, inhaling and slowly letting it out.
She brought the yoni.

Exactly, said Yolo, laughing.

They had sat in the circle talking for hours, as the moon rose
higher in the sky. During breaks some of them dashed across the
highway and jumped in the ocean for a swim in the moonlight.

Aunty Pearlua was of the opinion that it was time for men
to take another hard-to-keep vow in favor of children. She
thought they should resign from participation in any addiction whatsoever, even from drinking coffee and black tea. She
thought the example for the youth had to be clean, as she put it,
and extreme. No drugs, no alcohol, no "recreational" sex, no
caffeine, and no tobacco. She asked the men in the gathering to
make this vow.

It shocked them, Yolo could see from the look on their faces.
It was a look that said: Oh-oh, it has finally come to this. It
wasn't a look that doubted the wisdom of what Aunty Pearlua
was saying.

I don't think that can be done, said the blond man from
Australia who had confessed an addiction to coffee. He looked
stricken.

Behind every man's place in the circle were his "things." Car
keys, wallet, package of "smokes," and an unfinished bottle of
beer.

How can we do this? was the question that arose for everyone and led quickly to a depression of spirits.

But Aunty Pearlua was serene. She waved her fan around
the circle.

Do you think it's been easy for Mahus to conduct their lives as women, all this time? she asked. Don't you think from time to time we've wanted to cut off our hair and let our toenails grow long? She laughed. Ah, anyone can be a man, that is the problem. It takes much more to be a woman. But we have managed it. And why? Because we could see the plan men were laying out for woman and her children, a plan that enslaved and humiliated them before eradicating the divine in them entirely. Well, we Mahus were not going to have it. And you men today, seeing the plan laid out for our children, must say within your hearts: *We are not going to have it.*

It is an odd protest, someone ventured.

It is not a protest, said Aunty Pearlua. It is a strategy. A strategy for survival.

I've smoked since I was this high, someone else said.

Beer is my water, said another.

Our bodies are all we have, said Aunty Pearlua. Over our bodies we can have some control. We can make of our bodies exactly what it is our young people need to see. Health and well-being. *Freedom.*

Yolo cleared his throat.

Real men can't stop drinking, he said, sarcastically, under his breath.

Jerry looked at him sorrowfully. On this island that's pretty close to the truth, bradda, he said. We can't stop smoking or fucking around or beating our wives and kids either.

Marshall's brother, who everyone called Poi, was weeping; the sadness of his younger brother's death had hung over him all evening.

Finally he said: It's a good dream, Aunty, but it's too late. The shit comes into the islands by the boatload. Every fucking day. We can't stop that by not smoking.

And how do the cigarettes get here? asked Aunty Pearlua

coolly. You know how, they get here by that same drug-dealing boat.

Yolo was not the only one who had not expected this turn of events. There was a new energy in the circle, the energy of "if only." If only we had thought to try this, oh, maybe a century or two ago; if only we'd known about addiction when we were planting sugarcane and poisoning the weeds around it with arsenic before sending snow-white sugar out to enslave the world. If only Lili'uokalani had made her people promise to eat poi and taro leaves forever and not get hooked on white bread and processed cheese. If only the buck didn't stop here.

Our diet is a disgrace, said Aunty Pearlua. She snorted. Now, I admit I'm big, like a lot of these other big Hawaiians you see around here, but there's no reason for me to be this big. Except all the junk that now goes into this body. She made a face. All the white bread and mayonnaise. The beer. The smoke. All the pig and pasta salad.

That's our culture, though, someone said, respectfully.

No, it isn't, said Aunty Pearlua. Health is our culture; anything that interferes with it is our bondage. She grunted, and scratched her chin where the stubble was beginning to itch. I have Native American friends who are trying to talk their people off of fry bread, she said. It's killing them. All that worthless "enriched" white flour and grease. But they say, Oh, no, if you take away fry bread Indians don't have no culture. Such trash, she finished, and adjusted her lei.

It was at that point that an elderly woman with long silver hair and walking with a cane was seen entering the yard.

Aunty Pearlua got up from the circle to meet her. The two of them embraced, the elderly woman placed a lei made of green leaves around Aunty Pearlua's neck, and Aunty Pearlua kissed her on both cheeks. They returned to the circle hand in hand.

Though everyone else sat on the ground, a chair was brought for Aunty Alma.

She's real old, huh? asked Alma. My namesake?

Old and gorgeous, said Yolo, who had immediately wanted to paint her. She was small, plump, and brown, with large dark eyes. Her silver hair was thick and full and the breeze from the ocean lifted it gently as it blew. Her skin was very good, very youthful, and there was a radiance about her that captivated everyone. She was dressed in a long green dress that made her seem part of the ocean that had walked up on the shore. Her hair seemed part of the moon.

Between us, she said to the circle, my sister Aunty Pearlua and I have kept something real about our culture alive. She has taught generations of Hawaiian women the true hula, the dance of the traditions and of the soul; and I have worked to teach cleanliness of the earth temple, the human body.

Everybody is surprised that an old lady like me loves John Lennon's music, but I do. And one song in particular I like: "Cleanup Time." Because that's what time it is now, not only for us on these few islands but all over the world. In Africa, in Europe, in China. In Australia. In Indonesia. In Atearoa and Fiji and Tahiti too. And in America, *whew!* She made a face. We will have no future eating the slops the masters have brought, and furthermore clinging to them for dear life.

It is all about food, as I see it, she added. The food we eat, how good it is for us. And how efficiently we cleanse ourselves of it when it no longer is good for us.

Some of us are holding on to bad food we ate *years ago,* she said, *and the bad feelings that went with eating it,* I might add, without any idea that this is the easiest slippery slope to an early grave. Children, she said, seriously, looking into each of their faces, *we must learn to let go.*

It was so unexpected, this visit, this subject, that the circle was stunned.

Food? Constipation?

Suddenly Aunty Alma giggled. I see I have surprised you, she said. I like surprises, she said, impishly, don't you?

They didn't know you were coming, said Aunty Pearlua. They thought we'd be a circle of men.

Aunty Alma raised her eyebrow. Aunty Pearlua laughed.

When I Came Back Here

WHEN I CAME BACK HERE FROM NEW ENGLAND,
said Alma, dragging on a cigarette, I had a degree from one of
the best schools on earth; a degree in architecture. I wanted to
come home and build houses, beautiful, green, living houses,
like our ancestors had. I imagined every Hawaiian living in a
spacious house with a wide thatched roof, in which geckos
played and hunted all day, right next to a restored fish pond
from which they'd catch their daily fish. My houses would have
every modern convenience, of course, and be technologically
up-to-date. They'd have solar power, for instance, to generate
energy. She threw her hand toward the heavens. Look at all that
power, she said, squinting into the sun. Wasted.

Alma was so saturated with smoke and beer Yolo found
himself moving upwind.

And what happened? he asked. That sounds like appropri-
ate dreaming to me.

She stubbed out her cigarette on a rock in the yard and
promptly lit another. She looked at him with anger, hatred, futility, and sadness mingling in her face.

It's illegal to build such a house, she said, almost in a wail. I
tried everything. I even took people to court. They wouldn't

change the law. Look around you, she said. Do you think all these ugly prefab houses you see are an accident, or that nobody in Hawaii could have done any better? There are people dying to live again in houses that breathe, that interact with the elements, that let in some life. But they're outvoted and outmaneuvered by people who have deals with the construction industry on the mainland. So we get a lot of housing made out of pressed wood.

So what did you finally do? asked Yolo.

Alma laughed, bitterly. I got married.

I got married, she repeated, and I took the land my parents had left me and I used it to set myself up in real estate. By selling the land I was able to keep myself and my family going. But you know what I found out?

What? Yolo asked.

The land does not like being sold. It haunts me.

The land haunts you?

Yes. It is offended by my disrespect. It wasn't meant to be bought and sold, you know. It was meant to be loved and sung to; it was meant to be appreciated for its wonderfulness. And admired. Shared, yes. Bought and sold and abandoned over and over, no. Marshall and Poi understood this. I don't know how they got it, but they did.

Why is Poi called Poi? asked Yolo.

Because when he was a baby he would not take formula. I was so modern I was opposed to breast-feeding. He was just as opposed to Nestle's formula, which all Third World mothers were being sold. And one day, as I struggled with him, trying to get that bottle into his mouth, one of his flailing arms accidentally knocked over a bowl of poi. We were visiting one of my friends whose family still made and ate poi, and as soon as his fingers touched the poi he jammed them into his mouth. Within minutes he'd managed to eat up that whole bowl of spilled poi. And he'd done this without even opening his eyes. In Hawaii people have nicknames. Poi became his, instantly.

Yolo chuckled. He knew from the very beginning, he said. What was good for him. What was his.

They both did. They took to the land as if they'd always lived on it, and of course they had, but modern folks don't think like that. I was modern. Every time I sold a "property" they wanted to strangle me. And I was always selling to haoles too, which made it worse.

Alma, he said, reaching out to touch her shoulder, I'm so sorry.

So I play a lot of solitaire, she said. And I smoke and drink a lot. If I'm drunk none of it matters very much.

It matters to your namesake.

She doesn't even remember me, said Alma. She knew my mother, not the tiny baby my mother was carrying.

She doesn't have to remember you, in particular; she remembers the children of Hawaii, and you are one of them. She wants you to be healthy and happy.

I'm happy, said Alma, squinting through tears and drawing on a fresh cigarette.

On the Plane Home

ON THE PLANE HOME KATE WANTED TO CHEW GUM.
She thought she might have some in her mauve backpack, which
she'd stashed under her seat. As she rummaged through it looking for the gum, which she found squashed and linty, and which
she carefully unwrapped and chewed anyway, she noticed part
of a Post-it pad near the bottom of the pack. Taking it out she
saw it was the beginning of the story about a father and a
daughter she'd begun what felt like a century ago. When she
was running the Colorado. She began to read her scribbled dia-
logue. There they were, the characters in her story, trying to get
the father to eat after the death of the mother, his beloved wife.
Roberta, Kate's character, was finally able to get the old man to
eat. This had annoyed and saddened her sisters who had been
trying to get him to eat all afternoon.

Why had she written that? wondered Kate.

After eating the rice and vegetables she was served for
lunch, she sat gazing out the window of the plane, musing on
the mysterious nature of writing. All of it that had life was anchored in the dreamworld, she thought, but what had she
dreamed about? She suddenly recalled that this story had been
inspired by a dream of her mother after her death, who, in the

dream, had only one hand and with that one hand was untangling and then mending a net. Her mother's missing hand had grown back and she'd flung the net into the sea. *We do not need a boat for this,* she had said.

Kate remembered her fascination with the fact that her mother had regrown her hand.

As the plane carried her closer to her final destination, as flight attendants liked to say, Kate began to see all the pieces of the dream and the story clearly, as if a veil were being removed from her eyes. It came to her with certainty that she was not her father's biological child. That naming herself Roberta, after him, in the story was designed to reveal and to hide this fact. As was his way (to some extent in real life) of doting on her to the slighting of his own biological daughters, who were hurt by his attempt to make sure Kate felt like his child. Perhaps they knew! she suddenly thought; and experienced a wave of embarrassment that was like a hot flash. But then she thought that they probably did not, and that not knowing was even more cruel. For they would have believed he loved her more than them, and this they would never have understood.

That she was not her father's biological child was the reason her mother was always dissatisfied with her. Why part of her motherness was missing. It grew back only as She, the Daughter, resolved to look into Life for herself: *We do not need a boat* [a mother] *for this,* she had said, and: *The secret is, you do not have to be told.*

That explained why Kate looked so different from her sisters, so unlike her father. She didn't look like her mother, either. Maybe she was adopted? But no, she felt her kinship with her mother; they were alike in many ways. And they had identical heads of heavy, vigorous hair. Her birth was more likely the result of an affair her mother had had, during the early turbulent years of the marriage to her father, years the children had been told about. And she had come back from it, to "Robert," whom she loved, pregnant and filled with remorse.

Was it the *medicina*, the Bobinsana, that gave her this clarity? This certainty? It will make you see things in your life in a different way, Armando had promised. It will teach you to see through your own plots. Kate smiled, thinking of his warning. It is a plant, furthermore, that grows deep, deep, deep beside the river and remains where it is planted always. The river may change course but the plant will never move. When you drink it you too will want to root yourself, to find your riverbank and never uproot yourself again.

When Armando told them this about the Bobinsana Kate had had an image of everyone in America, the land of speed and movement, drinking it, and suddenly realizing they might as well stay where they are.

You could not tell me your beloved "Robert" was not my father, Kate wrote across the bottom of the Post-it. *He was my father, though.* She took the well-chewed gum out of her mouth and wrapped it in the Post-it; when the flight attendant came around again to pick up rubbish she pushed it into her bag. There, a paper curtain was removed! She felt things would flow much more smoothly with her sisters from now on. She would, in fact, share the dream, and its connection to the "story," with them, and ask them what they thought.

There were many subtle things she loved about her people, and how they bent themselves backward and turned themselves inside out in their attempts to love biological surprises was one of them. She thought of the half-European children hundreds of thousands of black women had delivered into the world, children forced on them through rape; children deliberately conceived in the bodies of black women so they could be sold. And they had pitied and loved these children; and in an attempt sometimes to prove it, they had seemed to love them more than their darker offspring. And what confusion had resulted from that! Still, the intention of the ancestors to cherish whatever the Creator shocked them with was noble, she felt, and good, and led to a people whose tolerance for the peculiarities of others was legendary. A tolerance they were sometimes denigrated for; but that was the bind and that was the freedom too.

She felt such overwhelming gratitude for her own parents that when the wheels of the plane touched the earth, she clapped to thank the pilot of the plane for delivering their child safely home again, then wrapped her arms around herself for sheer joy.

They Bombed

THEY BOMBED EIGHT DIFFERENT PLACES IN THE
world while we were gone, said Yolo, holding her close when
they met at Baggage Claim.

Okay, said Kate, with a sigh, resting against Yolo as if he
were a rock. I'm home now.

It did not seem possible that people would bomb one another rather than talk. What fear was this, that kept silent until
announced by the loudest sound on earth, the sound of worlds
being destroyed? Was it the fear that one's own terror would be
glimpsed, one's own childhood of terror guessed? She tried to
imagine any of her friends deciding to drop bombs on other
people. It would not have occurred to anyone she knew. What
would she and her friends drop instead? Food, blankets, matches,
tents, music. And she felt certain that if enough of this were
dropped, and all of it was cheap compared to the price of
bombs, the people who received the goods would in response
sell them, at a reasonable price, all the oil or whatever they required. As it was, a gallon of oil cost less in America than a bottle of purified water. So dropping goods directly to the people
from the air, bypassing all the middlemen who gobbled up the

aid sent through "official channels," made excellent sense. And what fun people could have!

The world was almost at the point of forgetting what a fine time people can have helping one another. That people like to work together and to kick back after work and share their expansiveness. What would happen if our foreign policy centered on the cultivation of joy rather than pain? she thought. She knew the answer; America would be the true leader of the world, not its biggest bully. So much of the world had thought America had a heart of joy, and had followed what they assumed was a lighthearted friendliness that made Americans envied and unique. Now they were seeing the other side. Well, as an African-Amerindian woman from the South she was intimate from birth with America's mean-spiritedness. The people who had lynched and charbroiled black people and cut open black women's bellies for sport had not died out and disappeared; they'd morphed into people who worked for the Pentagon and could do this sort of thing from the air.

You're dreaming, Yolo said as Kate talked about dropping bicycles and short skirts and jeans to women in Muslim countries.

Yes, she replied. As a woman, I have to. And she remembered a quote by the now thoroughly, in some quarters, discredited Winnie Mandela, "So far there's no law against dreaming." And of what had Mandela dreamed? Freedom from Nazi-Fascist oppression, labeled "racism" to make the native Africans somehow at fault. Freedom for her husband who had been in prison longer than they'd been married. And there had not been a glimmer of hope that anything would change in her land; and yet, because she dreamed, and because she encouraged everyone she met to dream, she had found her voice and so had they. And one morning her husband walked out of the prison beside her and became the country's president.

What happened to Winnie? Kate mused. Now everything one heard was negative; that she embezzled money, passed bad checks. Before that she had been accused of helping to murder someone. In photographs she seemed to be desperately clinging to youth, and to material wealth. Her dyed hair looked limp and lifeless, her eyes evasive behind expensive designer glasses, her fingers and arms and neck swathed in gold jewelry. The whole look of her was of someone lost. It made Kate weep, she had admired her so much. And yet, suppose the dream, the ability to dream, and to pass that ability on was all Winnie had to give them. It had been enough to see them, as a race, through many a dark and hopeless hour. It had brought to them collectively, the day her husband was freed, one bright and shining day. *Medicina* for a belief in a future. Thank you, Winnie, she said under her breath, and turned her eyes to fully appraise and appreciate her partner as they drove home.

Yolo was much slimmer too! He seemed more grave. His hair was longer and he wore it in one long plait down his back. A string of tiny flowers had been braided through it, but these had dried. Around his neck was a fat plumeria lei, a match for the one he'd pulled from a plastic bag and placed over her head when they met in the airport. Their car was perfumed, transformed into a magic carriage in which they sat like a king and a queen. Or like best friends. When he bent to kiss her as they stopped at a red light, she thought he tasted different. When she glanced at his hand on the steering wheel she noticed a new tattoo.

What's that? she asked, looking closely and lightly touching his hand. The tattoo was a short row of slightly curving blue lines, four of them, almost overlapping, and it was on the last digit of his pointing finger.

I got it last night, he said.

Did it hurt? she asked.

It sure did, he said.

They drove in silence for a while. Both of them happy to be homeward bound, happy to be safe and together. Looking forward to the night.

Later, in bed, he said to her: I loved eating supper with you (they had stopped to pick up the yummy Chinese vegetarian take-out they both craved); I loved being in the bath with you (she had emptied half a bottle of L'Occitane Ambre bubble bath into the tub); loved smelling and stroking you.

She grinned. It *is* good, isn't it? she said.

Amazingly, *yes,* he said, feeling her head settle on his chest. The world has never been in worse shape: global warming, animal extinctions, people fucked up and crazy, war. And then there are us, harmless little humans who somehow get to nibble at the root of things . . .

Did you meet any cute women? she abruptly asked. Or cute men?

It was hard for Kate to believe other people were completely straight, but Yolo was. He loved other men as brothers but why he'd want to sleep with a man when there were women around he could not fathom.

I actually remet someone, he said. An old lover.

Kate lifted her head so she could see him better.

And he began to tell her about Alma.

Her mother died when she was three, he said slowly, and she had breast-fed Alma from birth. When she died of influenza Alma was devastated. I can't even imagine how bad it must have felt. Suddenly to lose someone who loved you, held you, fed you from her own warm body. Her mother had been friends with an older woman who taught an ancient system of body purification. In fact, she had been one of Aunty Alma's students, and that was who Alma was named after. Aunty Alma is well-known today as a kahuna, or healer; the foundation of her healing is a cleanse. You fast for many days and among other things you do, you drink a lot of seawater. Alma, my friend, had never given her, or her gift to Hawaiian culture, a second thought. Well, said Yolo, when I got there, by some strange fate, I was asked to sit on a rocky beach beside the body of Alma's son. He'd died of an overdose of a drug they call ice.

Kate sat straight up in bed. No, she said, her eyes wide.

Kate, said Yolo, he was *so* beautiful. And he described the cutoff jeans, the beads around his neck, the earring. His name was Marshall. I asked Alma why he was named Marshall and she said it was because of the islands, the Marshall Islands, where he was conceived when she and his father had gone down there to try to halt the dropping of bombs the U.S. military was testing. Children there were being born without eyes or spinal columns. They were sometimes just blobs of tissue.

Kate was by now hugging her knees.

Yolo paused.

I'm going to save the rest for other times, he said, smiling into her stricken eyes. There's actually some good news. He kissed her forehead. Now you tell me something your crowd did.

And she, after a few moments of thought, began to tell him about the amazing plant, Bobinsana, that grew beside the river, whose roots, dissolved in water, she had drunk morning and night, and how she had begun to have dreams that diagnosed the illnesses of others.

It was funny to find myself coolly examining the innards of a bunch of people I had barely met; what wasn't funny was trying to tell them what I'd seen. She laughed. They didn't want to hear it. Fortunately nothing I saw was very serious. A hernia; a blood clot—well, I guess that could become serious, later on. A fractured clavicle that had healed wrong. I asked Armando the shaman: Should I tell or what? He thought it was up to me to decide, since I had been given the dreams. Anyway, she continued, the ones I told were only mad at me for a little while; then they forgot.

Forgot? asked Yolo.

You'd have to have been there, Kate said, and laughed. Try to imagine a bunch of middle-aged people sitting in a circle in the middle of the jungle, green with nausea, vomiting our guts out.

Do I have to? he said, laughing with her, and drawing her closer to him.

Neither of them said anything about sex, nor was there any movement that suggested making love. They kissed each other with their eyes open, before settling thankfully into the rich comfort of Kate's bed.

Sleeping with Yolo was always wonderful. He was warm and he smelled great. There was even something soothing about his snoring, which in the beginning had kept her wakeful and unamused. Her back curled into his, his arm curved under her breasts, there was a feeling of being snug and out of winter's way, even in summer.

They woke up the next morning talking.

And did I tell you, said Kate, that we got one cup of cereal and one banana per day? And not even a sweet banana.

I guess I shouldn't tell you about the lau lau and kalua pig, said Yolo. The pasta and a forgotten world of ice cream, Jell-O, and pies.

No, said Kate, don't.

And I was pretty much off meat too, said Yolo. But you know what? I couldn't say no to the people's food. I knew I wouldn't be eating it long, and it was very tasty. I also knew that to taste it was, in a sense, to taste them. They still cook pork in the ground, you know. They've been eating pigs forever.

Yeah, well, said Kate, I guess somebody's been eating grains and bananas forever. I got really sick of them.

But think how clean you are, said Yolo. I can taste it.

Speaking of taste, said Kate, you taste very different yourself and you smell even sweeter, if that's possible.

It's possible, he said, grinning at her.

Suddenly she realized what was different about Yolo. You quit smoking, she said.

Yes, he said. I'm happy about it too, he said after a pause, and while gazing intently into her beaming face, but to tell you the truth, sometimes I feel like chewing off my paws.

That bad, huh, she said.

I don't know if I can do it.

You can, she said. If other people do it, that means it's at least possible.

I really love smoking, he said. It's felt like a friend. I know it isn't, of course.

Yes, I know, she said.

I was so grateful you never minded kissing me.

I didn't, she said. You never tasted like an ashtray to me. And your oral hygiene has always been enviable.

I have a goal now, about quitting, he said.

You want to stay healthy and cute, she said.

Yes, he said, that too. But the real reason is that I took a vow, with a few other brothers of the world, to stop.

Yolo held up his hand and stretched out his finger.

These lines that you see are waves. There are four of them because most of the old cultures believe there have been four worlds, including this one. They are all connected by water, just as these tiny lines are. It is hard to see the connection, he said, peering at the end of his finger, but it is there.

How are they connected by water? asked Kate.

Because it is the same water. Different worlds, you know, destroyed time and again, but the same water.

Of course! said Kate, excited. Because there's no new water on the planet, it's all recycled. That means that when the Hopi sat out the destruction of the third world by living underground, when they came up everything was changed except the water. It had remained pure. They could wash in it, drink it, cook with it. And also, it had sustained them while they were underground. Water was loyal, she added, thoughtfully.

When I reach for a cigarette, or anything that would harm a child, I see my own finger, said Yolo.

Kate thought Yolo was of the bear spirit. The bear, according to ancient people who had known bears well, was of a loyal, generous, and young-loving nature. Bear mothers were the most dedicated parents imaginable. The most fierce in protecting their young; but also the most peaceful creatures when left unmolested. People with bear spirit had a certain feel about them: they often seemed large and strong, even if they weren't particularly. They gave off a vibe that made you want to sit near them. Not to talk, necessarily, but to feel. Yolo was like that. Kate had always loved this about him. Sometimes, as she'd sat on his lap, inhaling his bear-ness, she'd regretted the curl of cigarette smoke that cluttered her enjoyment of his fur.

Who am I without my smokes? Yolo asked.

Maybe someone who chews gum? said Kate.

Maybe someone who eats Hershey bars and gets fat, said Yolo.

Maybe someone who drinks a lot of coffee, said Kate.

Nope, said Yolo. That's going too.

No, said Kate. You love it so much.

I do, he said, but maybe it isn't love, maybe it's a chain.

Yep, she said.

Oh, said Yolo, the brothers got down.

You sure did, she said. What else are you giving up?

We said we'd try to think of sex as something really, really special, said Yolo.

That night Kate dreamed she was back in the Grand Canyon, right at the place where the Hopi claimed to have come up into the fourth world. She saw the little handprint, just as she'd seen it the day she was hiking with Sue. In fact, the person she saw standing near the little handprint looked like Sue, but when she looked hard she saw it wasn't. It was a Hopi man with a piece of rag around his head. The rag was dark; indigo, as she looked at it; wonderful against his bronze skin. He was wearing a long white cotton shirt, some kind of homemade sandals, and that was all. He said to her: *You have been puzzled about how we could live so long underground.*

Why would I be puzzled about that? asked Kate. *Everybody lives longer underground than above it.* She was thinking of dead people in graves.

The man was old but he didn't look particularly old. He

looked like he'd been the same age all his life. When he was a small boy, she felt, he'd been a miniature of himself. He'd probably always worn the exact same clothes too.

You have wondered how we sustained ourselves, he said. *And how we grew crops without sun.*

Now she noticed there were people standing in back of him. A woman of his own age and demeanor came to stand beside him.

We are never separate, he said, turning to the woman, who smiled.

We could never leave each other, she said.

A young man stepped forward. *In the night,* he said, *we came up into the fourth world to plant. We have never gone anywhere without our seeds.* He produced a tiny, colorfully decorated pot with a teeny hole in its top. *We carried our food, to last a thousand years, in a pot of this size.*

We made it, said the women, nodding at the little pot and standing behind the couple and the young man; *above or below, the earth is always abundant. To know the mind of clay, that is to know everything about survival.*

And when we came up, finally, to stay, we chose a place that looked like where we had been, said the older man. *That is why we have lived on top of mesas and had our fields far below. Where we live aboveground looks like where we lived so long underground. While underground we climbed up to plant, aboveground we climb down.*

You cannot get a grain of corn in this hole, said Kate, fussily. *You can't get sunflower seeds in here either.* On the other hand, she seemed to be saying this from inside the tiny pot.

All around her, as if in an echo chamber, she heard the people laughing.

She is very funny, one of them said.

And so tall, said another. *We must save her to plant another year.*

What was this thing about her and corn, Kate wondered. For now she seemed to be a very tall cornstalk. With big heavy ears of corn hanging off her like tits.

Corn used to be small, the older man said.

Really? said Kate.

Even so, we did not carry it in the little pot. It was always carried in a leather pouch, close to the heart.

Why was that? asked Kate, now back to herself, or whoever she was in this dream.

Because it is as dear as one's child.

Why is it as dear as one's child?

The world may lose corn, said the woman standing with the older man.

But perhaps its children are no longer dear, said the younger man, who had been joined by a woman his own age.

A baby materialized near Kate's feet and looked up at her. One of its legs was planted in the ground. A small cloud appeared right over its head and released a shower of rain to water it.

She awoke to the sound of moths. They were flying around the reading light she had left on near her bed. Not as large as the ones in the Amazon, they were still sizeable; white and silver and feathery gray. She studied them for a moment before turning out the light and going back to sleep.

I had a very Alice-in-Wonderland dream last night! she said to Yolo next morning. I was visited by the Hopi community that used to live in the Grand Canyon.

He was on his way to the gym. Cool, he said, flying out the door.

Yolo discovered that if he did laps, if he used the treadmill, if he took long walks and long naps, he could keep his mind off smoking, some of the time.

I am so nervous, he said at dinner, sitting on his hands as Kate ladled a bowl of soup.

Your knees are going up and down, yes, said Kate.

I feel jumpy, like I could jump right out of my skin.

Maybe there's a smoker's anonymous you could join?

No, he said, I want to do it a different way.

One night when Kate walked outside to see the new moon, she surprised Yolo, standing beside the hedge smoking a cigarette. When she came closer, she saw he was weeping.

I feel like such a failure, he said to Kate, not to mention a slave, as he bent to press the cigarette against a stone.

Kate stopped his hand. Then reached up and gently wiped his eyes.

Smoke it, she said, lifting his elbow so that the cigarette was near his mouth. Smoke it and enjoy every puff.

Taking his hand she led him toward a bench in the yard. As they sat, she said: I've always loved what Oscar Wilde said about temptation. That the only way to deal with temptation is to yield to it.

Yolo sighed.

What is it that you're smoking? she asked.

It's called American Spirit, he said. It's supposed to be natural tobacco, without toxic chemicals.

It smells okay, she said. I even like it. She breathed in some of the smoke. My grandfather smoked a pipe, she said; I liked to watch the white puffs come out of the pipe, mingle with the air, and disappear. When Indians smoked the peace pipe they didn't inhale. They pulled in the air, puffed out the smoke; air and

smoke mingled, and this symbolized oneness. *Being of one mind.*
That is peace. The material and the spiritual come together in
smoke, and the connection becomes invisible again almost immediately. Peace is as fragile as that.

You don't have to aim your mouth at the heavens, she said.
And you don't have to hide outside to smoke, either. I think we
should make a place for you to smoke beside the fireplace; that
way, most of the smoke will go up the chimney.

I still intend to stop, said Yolo.

Yes, well, until you do, said Kate, and reached for his hand.

They sat in silence, gazing at the moon and the slow arrival
of pale, barely perceptible stars.

After a while Yolo said: *I feel safe with you.*

And I with you, said Kate.

There was more silence.

I thought it was over between us, said Yolo. When you left,
I thought it was over. I was sad, but it felt final.

I thought the same, said Kate. I felt we were on different
journeys and that mine was so different from yours you'd never
understand it.

As soon as you left, I began to dream, said Yolo. I think I
started because as soon as you left I really missed you. The
whole other side of life had vanished, he said.

Yolo, said Kate, do you think we should continue journeying together for a while longer?

Yes, he said promptly, squeezing her hand.

In the old days, Kate said to Yolo next morning, kissing his
eyes before they got out of bed, at this point in the story there'd
have to be a wedding.

Well, said Yolo, we can have one.

But what would it look like? asked Kate.

There was silence. Every wedding image that came to mind seemed absurd. All those long gowns you couldn't run in and the veil that was a reminder of woman's captivity; still used in places in the world where the veil was made of fabric too dense to see through.

I'm never going to dress peculiarly to marry anyone ever again, offered Kate.

Oh, said Yolo, we've outgrown actual *marriage.* When I think of a wedding I think mostly of the feast.

The feast! said Kate, excited. Yes. And the circle, and the stories and the dance. And the three bears who are always invited in the end!

Yolo began to laugh. He was thinking of Aunty Alma, Aunty Pearlua, and Alma junior.

Kate was thinking of Lalika, Hugh, Missy, and Rick.

Rick said right away that he couldn't come, but Hugh, Lalika, and Missy said they would.

It's going to last three days, said Kate, over the phone. It will be near a river—we're trying to find one now. We will do ceremony and paint our faces with yagé and each of you must bring a story as your gift.

Can it be a real one? asked Lalika.

That's the only kind allowed, said Kate.

I've got a boyfriend, said Missy. I'd kinda like to have you look him over. Not necessarily look *inside* him. Can I bring him?

Sure, said Kate. And your mother too, if you want.

Nah, said Missy. We're not talking to each other. Maybe some other time.

I'm still sick, said Hugh, and I don't weigh much more than a straw. But I'm on these new drugs and I've come out to my family. I've even got a beau. Can I bring him?

Of course, said Kate.

Lalika asked if she could bring "someone." Kate said "someone" is just the person I want to see!

She and Yolo drove up and down the state looking for the right place.

Have you called aii your peopie? asked Kate.

He had.

Alma said she could come, along with her namesake! Yolo could hardly imagine seeing them together. And hearing the story of how that had happened.

Aunty Pearlua said she'd come, if she could bring the two brothers from Australia, who, she said, were studying with her.

Hula? Yolo wondered.

Jerry was coming, and Marshall's brother Poi.

And at last, after searching many days, Yolo and Kate found the perfect place, the perfect river. They found a campground north of where they lived, not far away at all, with small bungalows and an indoor cooking and eating area. In case of rain. There was a large firepit, circled by springy grass that would be great for sleeping and storytelling around the fire at night. And most marvelous of all, there was, visible from every place on the land, the most amazing, pure, deep, languidly flowing river. Its water so clear they could stand on the rocks above and watch rust-red salmon glide by. It was paradise.

You don't understand about Buddha, said Grandmother. *He would not mock those who take up arms against their own enslavement. Sometimes there is no way, except through violence,* to freedom. *Living in violence is not the best use of life, however. And he was interested in teaching that. How precious it is to have a human life to live! How sad to waste it in something so grim and blurry. A thought can be like a gun; it can slay the enemy. Music can be like a sword; it can pierce the heart of the enemy. Dance can kill. What needs killing is not the person; what needs killing is his or her idea that torturing another person will create happiness. When Buddha sat under the bodhi tree, he was sitting under Me. He was sitting under Me, she repeated, as tree. And he was sitting on Me as grass.*

When you drink yagé, you complain about how bad it tastes. It tastes bad because you have killed it in order to have it. This is not necessary. For the Buddha, it was not necessary. Sitting under Me and on Me, he received the medicina. *He did not have to groan and shudder and screw up his face,* Grandmother said with a rustling laugh, *before drinking something made of my dismembered body, and boiled over a slow fire. This is possible, receiving the* medicina *this way, if you open your heart.*

That is why people take the time to learn how to do that; open the heart. That is why they go on retreat. That is why they learn to meditate. The very poor, as you have noticed, rarely have this option. The moment they try to open their hearts, after slaving all week for someone who drains them of hope, the powers that be rush to implant a religion, generally foreign to their natures, into them. That is why I am happy to offer my dead body for them to eat or drink, and why my material essence, though not living, remains pure and good for them to use. That is also why my ceremonies take place in the jungle, far from so-called civilization, whose primary intent is to rid the world of the Wild. Which is another word for Me.

What are you writing? Yolo asked in the middle of the night. Actually it was close to dawn. Kate glanced at the little serpent clock at the side of her bed and noticed it was almost five o'clock. The serpent was an anaconda that carried the world, with the face of a clock, on its back. She'd spotted it among a collection of *curiosidads* in a gift shop at the airport, after leaving the Amazon.

Did I wake you? she said. They did not always sleep together. Yolo had his own room, sometimes referred to as "the lover's room," across the hall.

I felt the bed shaking, he said.

Kate had been writing on her laptop, something she'd never done before in bed. She'd resisted the feeling of being in bed with a machine.

I'm writing what I can remember of what Grandmother Yagé taught me, she said.

How's it going?

Rough, she said, her fingers limp on the keyboard, her eyes fixed on the screen.

So much happened in those seven hours. I felt I learned more than I had in my whole life up to then. But it is such a different way of learning, of being taught. After we were brought out of Grandmother's presence by Anunu and sat having tea and a slice of toast to settle our stomachs, I sat there stunned speechless by what I had experienced. I thought I'd never forget a single thing. But by the time we finished our tea it had started to fade. I asked Anunu about this. She said it was the same for her, and that in the beginning she'd felt bereft, to have been shown so much and to have been patiently taught so much, and then to feel it evaporate. But she'd realized the teachings simply became a part of her. They became hers.

And do you feel that way? asked Yolo.

Yes, said Kate. To some extent I do. But I'm a writer; I want to manifest the experience; I want to see what it would look like as art.

She sounded unusually passionate for five o'clock in the morning.

Yolo laughed. *Okay,* he said.

Kate looked at him. The truth is that I miss her. Grandmother. I miss her terribly.

What was she like? asked Yolo. Though Kate had described her many times before. He liked being told about Grandmother the way a small child likes to be told about angels. He sank farther under the comforter and wriggled his toes a bit.

She was so *loving,* said Kate. And *patient.* But *brisk* too. *No nonsense about her.* And she didn't focus much on what was *wrong.* It really was like sitting in the lap of a gigantic tree, breathing together, and accessing a *knowing* that would never happen in a high-rise apartment building.

She's more like: This is like *this* because that was like *that.* He did *this* because earlier he'd done *that.* She acts like *that* because where she's from nobody understood *this.* And the main thing is that she makes you see that the magic of the mystery we're in just goes on and on. After all, you realize you're sitting there, enthralled, being taught by a plant. There is no end to wonder! Yolo, imagine. Even if we live forever, we'll never get to a place where we can honestly say: There's nothing happening here; I'm bored. Or, you can be bored, I guess, but you can never say it's because nothing is happening. Something is always happening. In fact, *everything is always happening.* It's *amazing,* she said, closing her eyes.

Gosh, said Yolo, you really make me want to try it.

It tastes like shit, said Kate. You'd hate it.

How ironic, said Yolo. Something so good tasting so bad. But life is like that too, sometimes, he added.

She decided to tell him about the last part of her time with Grandmother, which she remembered clearly in every detail. But first she had to admit something to him:

Yolo, she said, I think I went searching for Grandmother because I am afraid of growing old.

I've always thought you very brave, owning up to your age as it comes, said Yolo. I also think it's natural to feel apprehensive. We live in a culture that is afraid of old age.

I know, said Kate. What I didn't know was that I too had this fear. I thought I had escaped it somehow.

Yolo chuckled. How can you escape when every commercial you see advises you to *hate the gray, hide it away.*

I almost couldn't see a point to living beyond middle age, said Kate. I mean, what is there to do, after that? Had anyone told us?

We could "retire," said Yolo.

Yes, said Kate, and enjoy "hobbies."

I can't imagine having a hobby, said Yolo.

I can't either, said Kate. Everything I do I want to be essential.

After seven hours with Grandmother, said Kate, I finally got right down to it. I was in this huge jungle, not unlike the Amazon. I was going all over the place desperately calling for Grandmother. My voice was as weak and desperate as a child's. I was beginning to sniffle a lot and I think my nose was probably snotty. Grandmother! I called. *Grandmother!* There was a deafening silence. The trees all around me were enormous. It was an ancient forest, with old trails hacked through it and trod by human beings, perhaps for millions of years. But where was everybody now? Absent. And in this primeval landscape I was calling for Grandmother until I was hoarse and on the point of tears. Because it was coming to me with a horrible certainty that I was by myself in this frightening place and SHE WAS NOT THERE! My heart sank. I had never felt more alone in my life. And then, just when I was on the point of dying of loneliness and lack of direction, I wailed: *Oh, Grandmother, you are not here!* And she said: But *you* are.

Kate smiled at Yolo, and wiped a tear from her eye.

The buck stops here, she said.

You are Grandmother, said Yolo.

Yes, said Kate. I thought I could avoid it, I guess.

There were hours of instruction like this, she continued, with pictures to illustrate everything; this is the only one I recall so fully. But in a way, this is the only one I need to recall. What she showed me was, Yes, I am Grandmother as she is; there is no separation, really, between us. And that, on this planet, Grandmother Earth, there is no higher authority. That our inseparability is why the planet will be steered to safety by Grandmother/Grandmothers or it will not be steered to safety at all.

Raging Grannies, said Yolo, Gray Panthers.

No, said Kate. *Grand Mothers.* We must acknowledge and reclaim our true size. Dignity is important. Self-respect. We cannot lead by pretending to be powerless. We're not. Age is power. Or it can be if it isn't distracted by shopping and cooking and trying to look nineteen.

Or tripped up by Alzheimer's, said Yolo.

Or buried in nursing homes, said Kate.

Don't Go Anywhere

DON'T GO ANYWHERE, GRANDMOTHER HAD SAID. YOU *are already out in space. If you go to another planet you will by your presence contribute to its loss of integrity. You will spend all of earth's resources trying to change a place that worked very well without you. Because you are vain, you will think you are bringing something useful. You are not. Look to your history on this planet; you have never brought a greater good, no matter where you traveled. That is because what is good is integral to itself. That is also why it is not worthwhile to change yourself, your hair or skin or eyes. What is integral to you will always be surperior to what is tacked on, simply because it is yours.*

There are space kin, beings from other planets, already on earth. They have been mistreated, or murdered, or hidden away. Earth has been visited by beings from other realms for a very long time. It isn't simply a fantasy that a few earthlings have conjured.

In fact, the first beings who came to earth were fleeing catastrophe on their own planet. They were running for their lives. They came to earth to hide. They hid in everything. Rocks, rivers, humans—when they appeared—animals and plants of all kinds. They are that which we say is the same in all things. They were very small, of course, invisible to the naked eye, not that there was a naked eye to see them at the time of their arrival, and they looked like very small snakes.

It had taken Kate a week or more, when she was in the Amazon, to notice the visitor to her hut every few days, a serpent whose coloring blended perfectly with the damp umber of her dirt yard. It was small and, according to Cosmi, who pointed it out to her, harmless. It still scared her.

Don't worry, he'd said. This kind of serpent will not come inside. Unless, he said, smiling, you are keeping small rodents or tasty large bugs.

It also followed a ritual: In the morning, after Kate had washed herself in the green water Armando gave her, and after she'd had a moment sitting quietly by the river, she could count on seeing the little serpent as she came back up the hill, just at the edge of the yard. It lay partly in shade, the jungle huge behind and above it. It seemed to be testing her.

Will she throw a rock at me? it seemed to ask.

Will she take up a stick and chase me away?

Well, no. She was not permitted to harm anything on this journey. Nor was she inclined to do so. She did keep her distance, though. And she did begin to carry a stick, though she never so much as pointed it in the snake's direction.

What does it mean to be completely outside the circle of goodwill? That was the question that came as she contemplated the snake.

Because of religious indoctrination, almost everyone feared and loathed the serpent. What damage had such hatred done to it; a magical expression of Creation? Was this, the banning of the serpent from the circle, the beginning of separation? Was this the model for all the other banishments? Hunted and killed, or killed instantly, on sight, forced to hide at all times, what did the serpent think of humanity?

Why had women, long ago, befriended the serpent, loved it? Why had Cleopatra had asps as pets?

Kate tried to imagine the lack of revulsion. It was surprisingly hard. She thought of the priestesses who had danced with snakes, sculptures of whom she'd seen in museums.

Maybe ancient woman thought the feel of the serpent's body was enchanting; cool and sleek and undeniably beautiful, as it was. And it could drop an old skin when it was outgrown! Maybe to her the feel of the serpent's body was like that of a cat to woman today. And Kate tried to imagine the cat being placed outside the circle as the snake had been, and the dread of cats humans would feel.

Black people had been cast outside the circle of goodwill for hundreds of years. This was perhaps the root of her feeling of kinship with her visitor. She saw how, as Africans rejoined the circle of humanity, so many carried scars too horrific to bear. Many of them, like women who lived in cultures that despised and willfully obliterated the feminine, would never experience the connection to earth and to humanity that was their birthright. Pain had driven them to separate from their very selves.

One Day, Standing in Her Garden

ONE DAY, STANDING IN HER GARDEN, KATE WAS surprised to see Armando coming through her gate. As soon as he saw her his face lit up in a smile.

Armando! said Kate, rushing to embrace him. What are you doing here?

Behind him there were others, two women and seven men.

I have come to see you, he said with a shrug, laughing.

He was wearing faded khakis, a black T-shirt, a burgundy polyester jacket, and a green baseball cap. On his feet were new tan sneakers.

The other men were dressed similarly, even the white man whom Armando introduced as Charlie. Charlie's wife, Rela, was not white; she and the other woman, Lila, looked very much alike. They had dark hair and brown skin and bright, if somewhat sleepy, eyes. As introductions were being made, Yolo came from the shed behind the house that he'd been using as a studio, and Kate invited him to join them.

We've been traveling a long time, said Armando, after Kate had brought chairs for everyone and settled them on the porch. Sipping the water and juice she brought out on a tray, her visitors began to relax. She noticed that the men, every single one of them, except Charlie, kept looking up into the trees.

That's a fat one, one of them said in Spanish.

Um-hmm, said another.

Charlie explained to Kate that gathered on her front porch were eight of the most powerful shamans of South America. They had come out of various jungles and mountains and plains of their countries and were on their way to Washington, D.C.

We tried to call you, he said, but your number isn't listed and Armando lost the paper you gave him when you were visiting him. He remembered the name of your street because it is the name of his brother. He also remembered you told him your house was blue. It is the only blue house in the neighborhood. Once we found the street, it was easy to spot.

Kate laughed. My neighbors hate it, she said.

Ah, *vecinos,* said Armando. They never understand that the *medicina* they are needing is always arriving, and moving in next door to them. It looks strange to them and they are afraid to take it.

Grandmother told me I needed to live in space for a few years. Yolo, my partner, painted the house. My neighbors think it is not earth-colored.

It is blue, planet earth, said Armando, surprised, and as if this should be obvious. Do you realize this probably helps us avoid assaults from space neighbors who are warlike? Because we are blue, like space is blue, we have disappeared from their screen. Anyway, he said, the truth is that at a certain point in one's spiritual development living in a blue house is imperative, whether Grandmother suggests it or not. It is a color that suggests the infinite, and the soul wants to live there because it is the most free place to live.

There are in fact three colors that the evolving soul encoun-

ters and must eat: the color of earth, literally dirt, which includes all the browns and tans and yellows; the color of men-
strual blood, which includes the reds, oranges, and maroons;
the color of water and space and eternity, which is blue.

You will see when you travel, said Armando, that in every
community someone will be living in a blue house. That person
you will find is somehow different.

Among Buddhists, blue is the color of healing, said Rela,
speaking for the first time.

What does it mean to "eat" a color? asked Kate.

Oh, said Armando, think of how you feel when you enter
your gate and feast your eyes on this color. There is a joy that
you feel, no? A lifting of your spirit?

Yes, said Kate. I certainly do feel that way.

Well, said Armando, it is as if your blue house is a big cake
and your soul, seeing it, takes a big delicious bite. It must be
awake to eat the color; when it is awake enough to eat the color,
it is a healthy soul. Many people cannot eat the color blue; and
they haven't digested their reds and yellows either.

A pharmaceutical company is trying to patent yagé, said
Charlie, when Armando finished speaking.

Patent Grandmother? said Kate, incredulous.

Yes. Well, said Charlie, they have stolen everything else indigenous people have developed for healing.

But to patent Grandmother, said Kate. It would be like
patenting a human being. Or life.

They'd like to do that, said Armando. But we are optimistic.
We will go to Washington and talk to your leaders. We will
make them understand yagé is a sacred substance. It is inseparable from spirit. It is also inseparable from us, the people who
are its neighbors, who have lived and interacted with it for
thousands of years.

By now the other male shamans who did not speak any English, and very little Spanish, had moved off the porch and were
walking about the yard. Looking up the whole time. The
woman shaman sat quite still, watching them.

Yolo looked at Kate and raised an eyebrow.

Then it occurred to her: These were men who spent most of
their time in the jungle, hunting. To them her large oak and fir
trees were *canopy;* they were watching her squirrels.

One of them said something; all the men, including Armando and Charlie, laughed.

What did he say? asked Yolo.

He said, said Armando: Where is that blowgun when I
need it!

Kate and Yolo joined the laughter. It was hilarious to think
of eight serious shamans/hunters fantasizing about her plump
city squirrels.

Armando and Charlie and Rela explained they hoped Kate
would write a letter saying she knew Armando and also knew
the value of yagé to its people. They would take this letter with
them to Washington, D.C. Kate said she'd be happy to do it and
went immediately to her study.

While she wrote the letter, Yolo invited everyone inside, and
Charlie, who had worked with the shamans for many years,
helping to preserve their medicinal treasures, showed a video of
a meeting of all the shamans and South American elders that
had taken place a few months before. In this video, some of the
wisest people on the planet shared their views on the ethical use
of such a powerful human ally as Grandmother. After Kate finished her letter she came to watch the film. Her TV monitor was
in the guest bedroom, which was small. All eight shamans, plus
Charlie, Yolo, and Rela, had crammed inside, five of them on
the bed. It was a sight that moved her to tears.

She remembered sitting with Armando one morning in the Amazon and almost being afraid to tell him the yagé had ceased to work. But he had not seemed perturbed. Sometimes Grandmother is like that, he had said. Maybe she has other work for you to do.

Kate had sat looking toward the river. She had come all this way, she thought, and like the guru of Ram Dass, who had taken a ton of acid, the *medicina,* in this setting, right where it was born, did absolutely nothing.

Armando was looking at her with shrewd eyes.

I think you have an idea of what you are to do, he said.

Oddly enough, she did.

Well, she said slowly, as you know, during my first visit with Grandmother, I was given seven hours of astonishing instruction. In a way it is greedy of me to ask for anything more. I think I'm here to meet her; to understand where she's from. To see her living body before it is cut; to see the people whose health often depends on her. I am meant, I believe, to be her friend. And to be yours.

Armando did not reply, but merely nodded his head.

Squeezing into the room now, Kate found the only available space to sit was on the bed. As they watched the native elders of the Americas gather to protect the inheritance of all who can be taught and healed by the plant magic of earth, Kate savored being in bed with so much wisdom. She marveled at the unwavering dedication of the shamans. That they had come so far, dressed so thinly, to defend Grandmother's *medicina* and its curing of the sick.

Yolo and I are calling a circle to celebrate sharing our life together, Kate said to Armando as the shamans were leaving. We'd really love it if you could come.

I would be honored to come, said Armando. But, *la vida*

being what it is, who can say? If I do not make it, I will send a spirit to take my place.

Not a jaguar, said Kate, laughing.

No, said Armando, I will send something small, something that loves humans, something trying hard not to be afraid.

After shaking hands and embracing, everyone left, Yolo and Kate waving from the gate.

It Will Be a Long Time

IT WILL BE A LONG TIME BEFORE HUMANS LOSE THEIR terror of me, said the serpent. *Though this serpent shape, this slithery form, is buried deep in every cell of every person on earth. It is the fundamental shape that is common to all. It is the shape of your DNA.*

In the dream, Kate had just sprayed poison on a toiling pile of ants that seemed to be living in one corner of her house. It had not seemed the right thing to do, yet the infestation unnerved her. As she looked, however, she saw each individual ant growing *larger.*

How are we to deal with fear? she asked.

How else? said the snake, smiling benignly, like Mr. Clean from the Buddhist retreat she'd left an eternity ago. *Make friends with it.*

That's what the Buddha taught! said Kate, shocked to hear the same instruction coming from a snake.

Yesssss, said the snake. *He was in alignment.*

It Was a Warm Sunny Day

IT WAS A WARM SUNNY DAY IN AUTUMN. IN TWO days Kate and Yolo would join their friends beside the clear, beautiful river they'd found in the north. Everyone was coming; the women from Kate's women's council; the men from Yolo's Sangha. Their friends from Hawaii and the Amazon. Avoa and Sue and Margery from the run of the Colorado. Anunu and Enoba. Even Rick had called and said he'd be coming. That he had experienced a breakthrough. He was so excited he kept repeating: I'll be on American, Flight 911, even after Kate told him that no one would be there to meet him, that he'd have to arrange transportation himself.

Yolo cleaned up his studio and swept the yard, and Kate swept out and saged the house. When she finished she went into her altar room. Everything was just as she'd left it more than a year ago. Buddha was still under the purple cloth. Her parents' pictures were turned to the wall. Che and the Virgen de Guadalupe were in a corner. The rolled-up poster of Quan Yin had a spider nesting inside. She uncovered Buddha. Very carefully she began to dust each photograph and to put it back, just where it was before. Soon her altar, with its pregnant, barefoot Third World woman, Bessie Smith and Lester Young, its candles and a pair of baby shoes, a red clay pipe and fresh flowers from her garden, looked just the same as always. She studied it carefully. What was missing?

Yolo came in and Kate handed him a box of matches. He began to light the candles until they illuminated the room. They sat on cushions facing the altar, enjoying the scent of sage and the candles' golden glow. Feeling connected and at peace, they fell into meditation without signal or plan. When they came out of it, half an hour later, Yolo went into the kitchen and returned with a small bowl of water into which he'd poured salt. This he placed on the altar near the flowers. Kate went to the refrigerator and took out the half bottle of yagé Armando had given her, which, at the river, she would use to paint the faces of her friends. She placed it between Che and the pregnant woman. Next she went into the living room and dragged the tall potted ficus close enough for its branches to gracefully shelter them as they sat. Finally she went to her bedroom and got the anaconda clock. Giving the anaconda a kiss and not looking at the time, she placed it in Buddha's lap.

Afterword

There is a magic intoxicant in northwesternmost South America which the Indians believe can free the soul from corporeal confinement, allowing it to wander free and return to the body at will. The soul, thus untrammeled, liberates its owner from the realities of everyday life and introduces him to wondrous realms of what he considers reality and permits him to communicate with his ancestors. The Kechua term for this inebriating drink—Ayahuasca ("vine of the soul")—refers to this freeing of the spirit. The plants involved are truly plants of the gods, for their power is laid to supernatural forces residing in their tissues, and they were divine gifts to the earliest Indians on earth.

—*PLANTS OF THE GODS:*
Their Sacred, Healing and Hallucinogenic Powers,
Richard Evans Schultes, Albert Hofmann, and Christian Rätsch

Thanks

For their inspiring lives of curiosity and dedication I thank master *kumus* Margaret Machado and Glenna Wilde, of Hawaii; Don José, of Peru; and ethnobotanist and preserver of ancient medicine Mark Plotkin, of New Orleans. For their legacies, their books, their talks, and their generosity in sharing knowledge and experience, I thank Maria Sabina, Richard Evans Schultes, and Jeremy Narby, whose book *The Cosmic Serpent: DNA and the Origins of Knowledge* contributes important insights to our time. I also thank Michael Harner for his ongoing work in the study and interpretation of shamanism, and Terrence McKenna, whose *Food of the Gods* offers a radical and rather cheerful vision of human development, deeply influenced by our primordial use of entheogens.

Kuma = teacher (Hawaiian)

Entheogen = Goddess/God within

ALICE WALKER won the Pulitzer Prize and the American Book Award for her novel *The Color Purple*, which was preceded by *The Third Life of Grange Copeland* and *Meridian*. Her other bestselling novels include *By the Light of My Father's Smile, Possessing the Secret of Joy*, and *The Temple of My Familiar*. She is also the author of three collections of short stories, three collections of essays, six volumes of poetry, and several children's books. Her books have been translated into more than two dozen languages. Born in Eatonton, Georgia, Walker now lives in northern California.

ABOUT THE TYPE

This book was set in Sabon, a typeface designed by the well-known German typographer Jan Tschichold (1902–74). Sabon's design is based upon the original letter forms of Claude Garamond and was created specifically to be used for three sources: foundry type for hand composition, Linotype, and Monotype. Tschichold named his typeface for the famous Frankfurt typefounder Jacques Sabon, who died in 1580.